A LONG NIGHT'S STORIES

A LONG NIGHT'S STORIES

RUDOLF DOBIÁŠ

FOREWORD BY
Michael Žantovský

AFTERWORD BY
Tibor Žilka

ANTHONY EYRE
MOUNT ORLEANS PRESS

First published in 2018 by Hlbiny, s. r. o Lovinského 12, Bratislava, Slovakia.

Hlbiny wishes to thank the following for their support and cooperation: Anton Baláž, Jonathan Gresty, František Mikloško, Miroslav Pollák and Klub nezávislých spisovateľov (The Club of Independent Writers, Bratislava).

This edition published in Great Britain in 2023
by Anthony Eyre, Mount Orleans Press
23 High Street, Cricklade SN6 6AP
https://anthonyeyre.com

SEKYRA FOUNDATION

The Publisher wishes to thank the Sekyra Foundation, Prague, and Mr. Ivan Šesták for their support in the publication of this work.

© Rudolf Dobiáš, 2018, 2023
Foreword © Michael Žantovský 2023
Afterword © Tibor Žilka, 2018, 2023
English translation © Heather Trebatická 2018, 2023
English translation of poems © John Minahene 2018, 2023

Rudolf Dobiáš has asserted his right to be identified as the author of this work in accordance with the Copyright, Designs and Patents Act 1988.

ISBN 9781912945405

A CIP record for this book is available from the British Library.

All rights reserved. No part of this book may be reproduced or transmitted in any form or by any means, electronic or mechanical including photocopying, recording or by any information storage and retrieval system, without permission from the copyright holder in writing.

Printed in Poland.

CONTENTS

FOREWORD	7
MY LIFE	9
THE CELL	13
HUNGER	16
YOUNGER BROTHER	19
DEEP GREEN	67
POEMS BY RUDOLF DOBIÁŠ	151
UNSENT LETTER	152
THE WIND IN MID-NOVEMBER	153
WHERE ARE YOU OFF TO, MEN OF JÁCHYMOV?	154
YOUR LOVE	155
CONVERSATIONS WITH RÚT	157
THE WOMAN WAITING	158
HOME	160
THE HEART	161
FROM SPRING	163
AFTERWORD	165

FOREWORD

THE TALE OF GLOOM OF RUDOLF DOBIÁŠ

THE HORRIFIC TRAGEDY of the Soviet Gulag system had its lesser known equivalents in all the countries of the so called Camp of Peace and Socialism. Between 1949 and 1989, roughly 200,000 Czechs and Slovaks passed through the labor camps, 5000 died of the unbelievable hardships of imprisonment and 250 were executed. Only after the Velvet Revolution in 1989 did individual stories of these victims of communism emerge and became a part of historical record and oral history testimonies.

Like Alexander Solzhenitsyn in Russia, some of the survivors of this experience also left behind literary works, giving their stories the immediate plasticity and detail that hauntingly resonate in the reader's mind. In the Czech Republic, the works of Karel Pecka (1928 - 1997) and Jiří Stránský (1931 - 2019) represent perhaps the most comprehensive examples of the genre. Their Slovak contemporary Rudolf Dobiáš (1934), sometimes called the Slovak Solzhenitzyn, walked a very similar thorny path for similar reasons and at about the same time. Like Stránský, a member of a Boy Scout group, considered subversive and dangerous by the communist regime, he was tried and sentenced for the crime of treason and spent his twenties in the incredibly harsh conditions of the labor camps. And like Stránský, he began a writer's and poet's career after being released in the 1960s.

There, however, the similarities end. While Stránský writes about the will, the ingenuity and the friendship which enabled the inmates to endure the suffering, the persecution and the humiliations of prison life, Dobiáš delves all the way to the bottom of the pain and the desperation experienced by human beings subjected to cruel injustice and inhuman conditions. There is no earthly redemption in his stories, no absolution for the torturers. The transcendence of the almost total darkness present in his works is made possible only through his deeply held faith in the world to come.

In his best works, like the novella 'Deep Green' in this volume, a story of friendship, betrayal, loathing, despair, guilt and love against the background of omnipresent and anonymous oppression, Dobiáš explores the depths of the human soul like few writers since Kafka and Dostoyevsky, leaving for posterity an account and a memento to which no historical scholarship can adequately do justice.

Michael Žantovský,
Director of the Václav Havel Library
and a former Ambassador of the Czech Republic
to the United Kingdom, Israel, and the United States

MY LIFE

I WAS BORN on 29th September 1934 in Dobrá near Trenčín, (now a district of Trenčianska Teplá), into the family of a six-acre peasant who, in the course of the year, supplemented his income by working in a brickworks, a stone quarry or in the nearby sugar factory. My mother and father only had a basic education. After finishing elementary school in 1945 I earned a place at the State Grammar School in Trenčín, where I passed the state Maturita examinations in June 1953. From 1945 I was an active member of the scouting organisation *Junák*, which was banned in 1948. After grammar school I began to study Slovak and Russian at the Faculty of Arts, Comenius University in Bratislava. In that year I published several of my poems in the *Smena* newspaper. Three months later, in December, I was arrested and in August 1954 sentenced to 18 years in prison for treason. The main reason for my arrest was membership in an illegal scouting organisation, whose only activity was the production and distribution of anti-communist leaflets.

Once the sentence had been passed, I was transported to the Jáchymov district, where I worked as a miner in the Jáchymov uranium mines until May 1960.

In January 1961, after the 1960 amnesty, I had to enlist in an army technical unit. (Although the sixties are sometimes called "the golden sixties", even after the amnesty life was not easy for former Jáchymov prisoners and for us the sixties were far from "golden". We were still regarded with suspicion and our social isolation continued even after we had been released.)

During my two-year intensified military service—but without weapons, as we were too suspect to be armed—I gained the qualification of "road builder", which wasn't a great deal of help to me in civilian life.

In 1963 I married and took a job as a temporary worker in the Nováky coal mines. Applying for such work was the last resort after all the traumatic experiences I had searching for employment. I lived in lodgings, travelling home only at weekends, so I couldn't spend much time with my family.

Only after a year and a half requalifying as an ore miner did I get the opportunity to take a job as a manual worker in *Slovlik*, a factory in Trenčín operating around the clock to produce fodder yeast. There I worked until 1975, that is, up to my fortieth birthday.

The year 1975 was a turning-point in my life.

Even before finishing grammar school I had begun writing poems and when I left, I seriously dreamed that when I graduated from the Faculty of Arts I would become a writer. Prison and those years which bore its stigma following my release delayed my dream for a long time. But in 1975 I resolved once more to make it come true.

I went back to writing; first to writing literature for children and not only poetry, but also prose and fairy tales for radio. I was motivated to write partly by a newspaper announcement about a Slovak Radio competition for radio plays for children and adults as well as by a notice in a daily newspaper about a prose and drama writing competition for adults and children organised by the Slovak Literary Fund. I was successful in both competitions; sometime in 1975 Slovak Radio broadcast my first story for radio *Štyria bratia* (Four Brothers) and a little later Mladé letá published *Velké biele vtáky* (Big White Birds), my first book of short stories for young people. Thus began, if you will excuse me for saying so, my literary career. Since then I have written dozens of radio fairy tales, plays for children and young people, dramatizations of Slovak and foreign authors, as well as several collections of short stories for older children.

MY LIFE

In 1976 I risked a change and began to work freelance, and in 1977 I also at last became a "writer for adults". That year the *Slovenský spisovateľ* (Slovak Writer) publishing house brought out my first collection of poems *Slávnosti jari* (Spring Festivities).

These were not easy years, but I survived, while I supplemented my income by taking some less demanding employment; I spent several winters as a boiler man in gas boiler rooms and finally, in 1988-89 a friend of mine got me a job on the quiet as a warden for secondary-school children in a student hostel in Trenčín.

November 1989 saw the fall of communism. I remember that in those days I was so happy, I cried with joy. Since then a quarter of a century has passed and many people—those who did not experience what I did under communism—now say they are disappointed with the way things developed after 1989.

Of course, not everything that followed has been good. But the main things—democracy and freedom of expression—are still here. I—after what I experienced in my youth—will not hear a word against democracy and freedom, which I have at last lived to see.

After the fall of communism I began an entirely new life. In 1990-91 I became a journalist—I was editor of *Slovenský denník* (a newspaper founded in November 1989 by the Christian Democratic Movement, which hand in hand with the Public Against Violence movement (*Verejnosť proti násiliu*) brought about that great social change).

In 1992 I took early retirement. Since then I have devoted my time to writing. Between 1996 and 2009 I published several books of prose and poetry, in which I could at last speak out about my unpleasant experience of prison.

Since 2003 I have been living with my wife in my parents' reconstructed house in Trenčianska Teplá-Dobrá and in 2011 our son Vladimír and his family moved in with us.

Until 2013 I edited the journal of the Slovak Confederation of Political Prisoners *Naše Svedectvo* (Our Testimony). I have compiled four books of testimonies to the brutality of the communist regime *Triedni nepriatelia* (Class Enemies) and an Anthology of Poetry Written in Prison, *Básnici za mrežami* (Poets Behind Bars).

THE CELL

THE CELL IS the space between the door and the window. I can almost fill it with my own body. The journey from the door to the window is the shortest and at the same time the longest distance I'm allowed to cover—as often as I wish—during the daytime. According to my calculations, in sixteen hours a person in a cell can walk about sixty kilometres. The floor is flat and smooth, you don't stumble on it and you cannot lose your way. Nevertheless, from time to time I get the feeling that I'm going down, or the opposite—that I am climbing uphill.

Sometimes I am completely exhausted. You see, I am not allowed to sit down and I've got nothing to sit on. The bed, the little table and the board for sitting on can be folded away and so the guards' first chore after the wake-up call is, you could say, to make them unusable. After all, what if after an intense late-night interrogation I should want to sleep? Then this tried and tested interrogation method would be of no use. And so all I can do is walk. At first it is walking with my head held high—that is when sleep has more or less refreshed me and breakfast, consisting of a piece of bread and half a tin mug of herbal coffee, has given me strength, but as midday draws near, my strength wanes and my gaze drops to my feet and the floor; I keep looking at my soles, hidden in black cloth boots and my ankles, to see whether they are swelling up. I have no one to complain to or to ask for advice from. I am alone. Just before noon I at last catch sight of my own shadow on the cement floor. For a long time this becomes my only friend and it is possible that at that moment I would find no other in the whole world. But I cannot see his face. And then I realise that I haven't seen myself in a mirror for a long time. If someone held one up to me now, I might not even recognise myself. And if someone then ordered me: "Spit at the mug of that individual, that contemptible creature", I would probably obey them; I would spit at my own image, my forgotten likeness.

In spite of the deadly tiredness that comes over me during such an enforced walk, I look forward to another, also expected feeling: all of a sudden, as if some invisible, but impossibly taut wire has snapped, a strange feeling of relief, of lightness, washes over me. Not only have I shaken off the burden that was weighing me down, but I have managed to free myself from Earth's gravity, lift myself off the ground, and float above it. Perhaps this is the feeling one has at the moment of death. You live, although in fact you have already died. Or the opposite: you are dead, but in fact you are still alive. It all depends on the word order and maybe on the number of kilometres covered, on the intensity of the light in the barred frosted-glass window. And then one day the sunshine is even more subdued than usual. Not that it has grown dark outside, or that mist is hanging over the landscape you cannot see. The metallic ringing of the trams is as strident as ever and as unbearably provoking in its significance. My movement in the cell is the flight of Einstein's fly of relativity in a moving train. But in that tram there are people who are going somewhere, going to see or visit someone, they get off at the tram stop and continue on foot, or they wait for another tram, which—ringing its bell—announces its arrival from a long way off. These tormenting sounds and equally painful imaginings make me wonder why the light coming from outside is suddenly different, whiter, as if a million neon lights and milky bulbs have lit up and are flickering in the cold air like butterflies. No, of course they cannot possibly be butterflies, or May bugs, after all, it is the end of December; not long ago I mentally celebrated Christmas; I, Lazarus, who Jesus will yet free from the grave. So what is happening outside? It is snowing! Snow is falling; snowflakes are sticking to the wire glass windowpane, unbreakable and opaque, and perhaps they are trying to peep inside, to discover who that lone figure is staring at the blind window. They would be surprised if they saw me, as was that screw who brought me here. The interrogator had handed me over to him blindfolded with a towel, so he could hardly see half my face. And then when he took the towel off my eyes and saw I was quite a young lad, he shook his head at me incredulously for maybe twenty seconds. "So young and already such a swine," he finally remarked.

But that is all in the past. In the meantime we have got used to each other and the important thing is that snow is falling outside, the flying snowflakes have come to dance in front of my window and I can suddenly see them quite close up and I know they are not snowflakes, but angels; the sky is full of their wings. And nothing and no one can stop me joining them in that silent flight which, instead of floating down to the ground, is floating upwards. At that moment I become an angel.

So farewell, Mr. Interrogator!

HUNGER

AS A TEN-YEAR-OLD boy I saw a Soviet soldier, probably a Russian, die in my grandmother's yard. He had managed to jump out of a burning tank, but he was immediately mown down by a burst of fire from a German machine gun. Germans, and it is possible they were the same ones who shot him, carried him into Grandma's yard on a ladder. They put him down on the grass and hurried on. It was April and the Germans were retreating; they were trying to get to the River Váh and from there to Moravia.

The soldier had been shot in the legs and the abdomen. A neighbour, a war veteran and medic, came running up, but decided there was nothing he could do for the wounded man. The lad was very young, I guess not even twenty years old. He lay there dying for a long time, several hours, and while he was still conscious, he called out for his mother. It is said that all men call out for their mothers in their hour of death.

I was also very young, not even twenty years old, and I experienced not the hour of my death, but just a short period of hunger. I suppose I shall have to wait a while for my hour of death. The first hours of hunger are the hardest. Hunger becomes a craving as unceasing and obsessive as any other temptation. Eat! Eat! Eat! The commands from the brain are like poisoned arrows. However, they don't pierce the flesh, but the soul. They drive a prisoner mad. He can hardly stop himself from kicking down the door, tearing out the window bars or knocking a hole in the wall. Hunger reminded me that I was not free. I no longer spared a thought for the atoms of freedom; I was saved from madness by a little piece of bread, a tiny bit that I had put aside from my morning's ration for when things got worse. I divided it up into little crumbs, so that I could last out until the evening. I put the last speck in my mouth before my evening prayers. I had never prayed for my daily bread with such fervour as then, in the hour of hunger.

Fortunately, I was not deprived of sleep. Before ten there was a jangling of keys and the screw came to unlock my bed. At last I could stretch out. Sleep is the friend of the hungry and thirsty. The red-hot sword of hunger, which, surprisingly perhaps, burned in my chest and not my stomach, gradually began to cool down. What was previously gnawing at my insides like a disease, now changed into a headache, but even that soon gave way to a silent blackout. On the fourth or fifth day I experienced the first miracle. The red-hot sword had now cooled down completely and the gnawing beast in my stomach seemed to have found another prey, because its den in my insides was empty. And at that point I had no idea that in a couple of hours another miraculous event awaited me. It was in the afternoon, during the siesta, when the officers led the detainees outside for fresh air. The sun must also have felt like taking a closer look at me and so it had waited for me above the tiny exercise yard for undemanding and undeserving prisoners. My officer was probably angry with me, because a different officer collected me from my cell to take me outside. He was new to the job, though not some immature youngster but a man of about thirty, and he came four or five afternoons to walk me like a dog round the concrete enclosure, where there was never a living soul apart from the two of us. And during the whole of this time I was lucky with the weather. The sun literally squandered energy; every single one of my cells received its ration of warmth and light, solar sap swelling me to bursting point. I wouldn't have minded spending the night in this hot place; I would smell the acacia trees and howl at the moon; it was the end of May or the beginning of June and I was not even twenty then. However, each time I had to make do with the prescribed half hour; then the officer would blindfold me with a towel, take me gently by the elbow and in this way steer me towards the exit from the yard. In his company I obediently returned to my far smaller cage, deprived of the smells and sounds that came to me from beyond the concrete enclosure, but enriched by the sun's energy, stored in every particle of my emaciated body.

Eat! Eat! Eat! My famished cells cried out to me once more and that call must have been heard from outside too, because once when we were leaving the concrete enclosure, the officer secretly slipped into my hand two slices of bread which he had no doubt taken for me at lunchtime in the canteen for employees of the Ministry of the Interior.

"Hide them," he whispered. And when I had done so, he considerately blindfolded me and lightly pressed my forearm. The loosely tied towel allowed me to look down at my feet and thus for a few seconds more I could admire the tufts of pale green grass that grew in the cracks and crannies of the concrete bunker. The bread in the pocket of my brown, scratchy prison uniform was transformed into radioactive material; a thermonuclear reaction took place while I was still going up in the lift. However, it was me, not the bread that was changed; you see, that day I was satiated twice over, once with bread and the second time with human sympathy for my plight. It is said that at the hour of their death men call for their mothers. Sometimes, at the hour of hunger, you may also be helped by a stranger.

YOUNGER BROTHER

MY NAME IS Ján. That's the only name they called me by at home and at school; no familiar forms such as Janko or Jano could ever be heard in the meadows where we children used to play. Nor in church did the dean ever call me, his altar boy, anything but Ján. This was unusual in a village and to this day brings back the memory of my older brother, christened Tomáš. And how else but with an embarrassed smile can I entrust you with a little personal secret: that's not what my brother called me. Ever since I was very little he never called me anything but Shrimp. Tomáš was fourteen when I was born. I can imagine him bending over my cradle, shaking his head and saying, "What a little shrimp! I've never seen such a tiny kid in all my life!"

He called me that until the day he died. I didn't mind. I loved that word. I imbibed it with my mother's milk.

My father spent thirteen years in America. It ruined his health; he was employed in the ironworks and some foul stuff for cleaning boilers ate into his lungs; he fell ill, spent a year in hospital and then came home. That's why I am fourteen years younger than Tomáš. Five years ago father was declared an invalid; at least he got a job on the narrow gauge railway, because his pension wouldn't have been enough, even though he had worked for thirteen years in America.

So Ján it was. Ján—that has a proud ring to it—and for our needs it is enough to mention this detail. Those of us who avoid childhood memories for a thousand different reasons can at moments of early morning sleeplessness recall no more than that bullet-proof shell of morning sleep, but we hardly ever recall writhing in cobwebs woven by the spiders of our first dreams. I used to sleep in the front room in my mother's bed and Tomáš on the couch under the kitchen window, but when he was conscripted in '45 (I was six years old then and had just started elementary school), I persuaded my mother to allow me to sleep on the old sagging couch. In winter it was cosy in the kitchen and, as well as that, the window faced the yard and that was next to another yard, so an almost infinite space stretched before my eyes, where I could store secrets discovered almost daily by my attentive and at that time exceptionally diligent eyes. In particular these included rare species of birds that I sometimes only caught a glimpse of and that for the most part I dared put a name to only a week or two later, when I happened to come across someone like me who had not managed to crack this nut found under the tree of knowledge. Another reason why I'm mentioning sleep is the fact that I was the first to feel the chill (in both the real and figurative sense) that March morning when my Švošov uncle came down from the hills to bring my parents some news that for a long time they shrank from believing.

It was perhaps half or a quarter of an hour before midnight; the neighbouring houses slept the sleep of dwellings whose occupants had put themselves in God's hands. Because—and this should be emphasised—at that time, in '51, God was the only one people could trust. My uncle from Švošov was a slightly-built man, but the blows from his fists on the wooden gate sounded almost like the blows of fate, or at least that was how they projected themselves into my light sleep, immediately turning into a tangle of horrifying scenes and sounds. These woke me up. A couple of seconds later I realised that someone was trying to force their way into our house. And so, half asleep and half awake, I slipped my feet into the old boots I wore around the yard when it was muddy and someone had to give the rabbits hay or fetch logs from the woodshed. I quickly threw my mother's woollen shawl around my half-naked body (the thought flashed through my mind of how my classmates would laugh if they saw me dressed like this) and shivering with the multifarious fears of an eleven-year-old, I stepped out into the yard suffused in the shiny puddle of darkness. The door had hardly had time to creak when a sharp whisper came from beyond the gate: "Is that you, Ondrej?"

My father's name was Ondrej, and as I recognised the late visitor, I replied, "No, Uncle. It's me, Ján."

"Hurry up, open the gate! Open it, for God's sake, and go and wake your parents." It was not in the actual words, but in their urgent tone, like the hissing of coals extinguished in a hot, but invisible hearth, that with the sensitivity of a child I detected hidden danger. My hands shook as I released the bolt. My uncle shoved me roughly aside (I was probably in his way) and that shocked and grieved me for some time. I couldn't have any idea that Uncle was the bearer of a message and—as it later became clear—its interpreter too. Only later did I come to realise that grave events announce themselves from the very outset differently from ordinary occurrences. An occurrence could be said to be a one-off event, whereas the most important feature of grave events is their long-term effect. Fate knocks on the door in a different way to an uninvited guest. At that time, however, given my age, such thoughts could not have occurred to me. Bent strangely forward, as if searching for someone's footsteps in the house's hard earthen surround, Uncle hurried ahead towards the kitchen door. From the middle of the room he called in a hushed voice, "Mara! Ondrej! Get up!"

I had forgotten to fasten the bolt; I had to go back, which is why I missed the moment when my mother, dressed only in a long white nightdress, her hair hanging down on her shoulders, and my father in trousers and shirt, an emaciated apparition, appeared in the dark doorway. Gripped by a hitherto unknown anxiety, I slipped indoors like a timid mouse. Uncle was sitting on the couch, twisting his fur cap in his hands. He wiped his sweating forehead and neck with a large white handkerchief. I noticed that no one had thought to light the paraffin lamp, so I crept over to the stove, but when I struck a match, from Uncle came an almost inaudible "Leave it."

I sat down next to him on the couch. Warm steam rose from his unbuttoned fur coat. It seemed to leave a visible trace on the pale aperture of the window. In spite of this I was shivering with cold. As if he'd heard my teeth chattering, my uncle covered me with the feather duvet. But he still wasn't ready to come to the point. The oddest thing was that not even my parents dared ask him straight out the reason for his visit at such an unusual time. For a long time he went on mopping himself with his large white handkerchief; for a moment he bent forward, as if he was still searching for traces of something on the kitchen floor, and suddenly (with his head on his breast) he uttered a groan of such lonely and clearly genuine pain that it sent shivers down my spine. My mother sighed in relief. Relief! The event was probably tragic (after all, our relative wouldn't have come over the hills, especially at night, for no reason) but it clearly did not concern us directly. She sat down at the table to be nearer her brother, prepared to comfort him in his evident grief. She had no idea that this time her guess had led her down the wrong track. For immediately afterwards everything turned out to be quite the other way round. Like the contours of an unknown island rising from the dark depths of the ocean, the outlines of a story such as life hides in the last file of its data bank now appeared.

"They caught Tomáš!" announced our sweating uncle in the gruff voice of the false archangel.

"Tomáš?" I caught my breath in fear.

"Our Tomáš?" my mother cried out in disbelief.

"That can't be true," objected my father, not very convincingly. "They can't have caught him. He's in Austria."

"He came back."

My mother was the first to believe Job's news. She groaned. Her right hand moved towards her heart. Then she hid her face in her hands. She wanted to cry, but her throat was so tight, she couldn't. She sat up and her arms fell to her sides. Like this, she awaited the fateful blow. A moment of silence became a black patch on the white robe of eternity.

"Where did they catch him?" Dad asked resignedly.

"In Bratislava. There was a raid. He didn't stand a chance."

These words fell like stones and the night grew heavy with them. At last the clouds drew back and there was a glimmer of the moon. And the veil of the temple was torn before my eyes. Words drummed on the taut roof of my consciousness like hail. My thoughts had to encompass an infinite space.

One picture will be fixed in my memory for the rest of my life. I am looking at our reflection in the water. Tomáš is holding my hand. I hardly come up to his waist. The sun is bathing just a short distance from our heads. Its nakedness blinds us both. We are forced to turn our backs to it. The image is gone. Both the sun and we two have ceased to exist. It is the end of the world.

"Shrimp, listen carefully to me! I must tell you something."

"What?"

"Something I can't tell Mum or Dad."

(The whole of my being is alert. I feel I have grown up. At least my ears and eyes have grown bigger.)

"I'm leaving tomorrow."

"Where to?"

"The West."

(I realise for the first time that I am an inhabitant of the Earth. I feel the enormous space of the world stretching out inside me. A little way from me, at the tip of my shoes, is a dark patch of shadow. That shadow frightens me.)

"Why?"

"I must."

"The teacher said that's not allowed."
"That's exactly why I have to leave."
"Why because of that?"
"Because it's not allowed."
My bewildered gaze leaps from the tips of my shoes to the mirror in the water. I can actually hear the splash. The water hides everything. I shall come here every day and each time ask if it knows where my brother Tomáš is. Like chickens in the yard the words dashed around my brain: east, west, north, south. It doesn't make sense. I don't know what the cardinal directions are for. I fall silent. I don't know what else to ask him. The sun beats down on my head with its golden mallet.

Fortunately, I already knew where Austria was. I remembered who I had whispered it to first: "Our Tomáško is in Austria." Betka, of course. We used to meet behind the barns, in a world that offered itself as a friend and allowed us to enter No Man's Land, where apart from us only the Virgin Mary and St. Anthony could go. The little statue of St. Anthony stood on a concrete pedestal beside the lane that divided the backyards from the fields, and the picture of the Virgin Mary hung above the spot where we met and where, just like in Paradise, there stood a tree—an ordinary alder. "Austria is abroad," Betka had objected. "That's just it," I confirmed almost proudly. I carried Tomáš's photo around with me, where he was in his officer's uniform, having just finished the army academy. I showed it to Betka. She scrutinized the photo for a long time and then finally declared, "You don't look alike."

"Tomáško has fairer hair," I half agreed.
"But you have different noses."
"So what? We're still brothers," I retreated, perhaps into a blind alley I'd let myself be pushed into.

But now it was as if I had momentarily blacked out. It took me a long time before I began again to be aware of words and sentences that unlocked and opened hiding places inside me, of whose existence I had hitherto no idea, immediately locking them again with multiple locks of pauses and silence, clearly on account of my age. In the end my Švošov uncle suggested I should go and lie down, as I had to get up early in the morning to go to school and they needed to clear up a lot of very important things concerning Tomáš's arrest, and that was not for my ears. Offended and saddened, I couldn't even find the strength to protest and without a word I took myself off to my mother's bed. Ah, how humiliating it was for me to realise that I was excluded from the world of adults! It's a pity that my parents didn't understand that while for them the words "They've caught Tomáš" only meant what they literally meant and formed the basis for deciding what steps they would now have to take, for me this new situation would lead to a total change in my view of the world and life. I only had two possibilities: either I could decorate myself with the words "they've caught Tomáš" like an Indian with eagle feathers, or I could transform them into the deepest secret. In the end I succumbed to the latter like a bad habit, which eventually became both my secret pleasure and torment at the same time.

Although I tried my hardest not to, because I very much wanted to hear the adults' conversation, I soon nodded off. And when I awoke from a deep and surprisingly dreamless sleep, the daylight, still too bright for my eyes, was already shimmering beneath the trees. The pointed buds of the trees were willingly opening to the sun's rays. There was an aroma of coffee in the kitchen. Mum was moving soundlessly around the room, as if she was afraid to tread more heavily on the tiled floor. There were no sounds coming from the yard either. The explanation was simple.

"When you go to wash under the pump, let the hens out of the hen house," she instructed me when I had hardly entered the kitchen. The kitchen was tidy, the chairs pushed under the table, the black and red checked blanket smoothed over the couch, as if no one had ever sat there, to say nothing of lying there. It was a quarter past seven. Dad had already been at work for some time and Uncle most probably likewise: Dad for the forestry company, Uncle on the railway. I let out the hens, then went to wash under the pump. I ate a slice of bread and plum jam with my coffee. The jam was sour, so I sprinkled it with sugar. I expected my mother to give me a mouthful because of the sugar, but this time breakfast went without them. There was not even the usual question, "Have you got a handkerchief?" Mum's thoughts were elsewhere. I didn't feel like talking either. Even though the utterance, "They've caught Tomáš" was still valid, the moment I left the house everything seemed to revert to normal. But when on the way to school I met carefree classmates, many still with sleep in the corners of their eyes, I suddenly realised the abyss that had opened up between us in the night. We were no longer all alike. I had no idea, however, that my exceptional status would soon weight heavily on me.

In the village we had an elementary school with two classes. The teacher's wife was in charge of the younger pupils and the teacher taught the older ones. In those times villagers had respect for the teaching profession, which could not be said in later years. The teacher was a tall, thin forty-year-old with a narrow moustache under his nose. That day he made me feel embarrassed, for his gaze often wandered in my direction, but, in contrast to other days, he didn't call on me to answer even once. Before lunch, however, the anxiety I had been carrying around in my heart ever since the morning evaporated. I even laughed when Betka garbled some word and the teacher promptly made a pun of it. After lessons, however, the old anxiety came back. I didn't want to go home, where I should probably only have found my mother's silent shadow. I waited outside the school for Betka and on the way home I shared my tormenting secret with her.

"They've shut Tomáško up. Put him in jail."
"Do you know that for certain?"
"Yes."
"They catch some people and then immediately let them go," Betka

said tentatively. Her remark comforted me, as if I expected Tomáš's fate to depend on a young girl with rounded shoulders and a fair pigtail. Those words were good to hear. I could even have believed them, but after the war people in the village had already had prior experience. Kováčik's son had been taken captive by the Russians when the front passed this way and it was four years later that his family received the first letter from him, at Christmas. From it they learned that he was being held in prison in Russia.

"This is different," I said after a while.

"I think so too," Betka agreed, perhaps too willingly. Then we dawdled through the village without exchanging a word. It was a pleasant, sunny day, several goslings were cackling in the yards. I said nothing, even though my mouth was full of words. I felt relieved when Betka left me (she lived in a side street leading to the railway crossing). I felt lonelier, it's true, but also more self-assured. I didn't find my mother at home. Dad must have come home from work a short while before me. He was sitting at the table, sipping bean soup. I sat down opposite him.

"Where's Mum?"

"I don't know," he snapped.

It was already dark when Mum came home. We immediately surrounded her as if we wanted to chase away the foreign smells from her smooth face, still pale from the winter sun. Her hair smelled of warm spring dampness and when it slipped out of the white scarf with red flowers, it reminded me of the eel I had managed to catch during the previous school holidays.

"Where've you been so long?" Dad asked her, more grumpy than curious.

"At the National Committee."

"What were you doing there?"

"Old Rehák came for me."

Rehák was a municipal employee. He used to go round the village with a drum on his belly and sticks in his hands and his drumming enlivened and often woke up the village.

"Some secret policemen were waiting for me there," she added wearily.

Mum's reply made Dad jump up from my couch. "What did they want?" he asked in alarm.

"They were asking about Tomáš. And about some other people, whether I knew them or not. I didn't tell them anything," she declared, sinking down on a chair under an invisible burden. "So they left me sitting in an office for over two hours. There were three of them there with me: two young ones and a third about fifty. They smoked, gazed out of the window and from time to time one of them asked: "Well, have you remembered yet? We've plenty of time; we'll wait until you've grown tired of not saying anything."

"They came to see me, too," Dad said, as if just by the way.

Secret policemen! I felt something grip my insides: fear. The connection between my mother's absence and my Dad's remark produced in my imagination a white cinema screen. The word "secret policeman" had come up several times in the conversation between my parents and uncle. At the time I had imagined them as beings without bodies, spying from behind every corner on Tomáš and people in general. Now, however, they had been to see my father and had summoned Mum to the National Committee, so they were most certainly beings of flesh and blood and, moreover, someone must have told them where Dad worked and what he did. What if they should put my parents in prison? I wondered and wanted to cry. Dad noticed my lips trembling and he came over to me and ran his fingers through my hair.

"Don't worry," he whispered, but I felt that the ground had given way beneath Dad's feet too and I gripped his stroking hand tightly, as if we were both plunging into an abyss. "We've no reason to be afraid," he declared rather too loudly, glancing sideways at my mother. I realised that his confidence was only feigned. Because of me. We were all standing on an ice floe; it was cracking under our feet and breaking up into little pieces.

The next day, towards evening, a black car stopped outside the Kováčiks' house and two men in long leather coats and hats on their heads jumped out of it. A short while later they emerged, leading old Kováčik; he was only wearing trousers and a shirt and in his state of half dress, was pushed into the car. I saw it with my own eyes while hiding behind the fire station. At last I had seen secret policemen with my own eyes! That evening they came twice more, for Markuš, Slezák and Mičiatko. No one knew why they were being taken away. All three worked in the textile factory. Their wives and children were crying; Mičiatko's wife even struggled with the policemen. The Mičiatkos had five children; they were all outside, wailing. Mrs Markušová on the other hand clung to her husband's arm and wanted them to take her too. Old Zúber, Slezák's father-in-law, who had lost a leg in the Uprising[1], cursed the secret policemen, calling them Gestapo and SS men, but they left him alone. Mum lit a candle before a statuette of the Virgin Mary and chanted the rosary. Dad got a fit of shivering and had to go and lie down.

The next day it was as if everyone had been struck dumb. Life in the village was like a stream covered with ice. You had to break through it to learn the truth. The truth crept up to me on tiptoe too, because even truth can be considerate, especially to children.

Further stories of Tomáš's arrest arrived in the village together with the swallows. But they seemed to be written in water and were like heavenly signs, because there was no clear explanation for them. For several more days, perhaps even weeks, we seemed to disregard the unpleasant truth, postponing it like the extraction of a tooth or some other painful necessity. Then the postman brought a postcard in which Tomáš wrote to ask us to send him a toothbrush and toothpaste. Address: Bratislava, and

---
1   The anti-fascist Slovak National Uprising of 1944

P.O.Box. And a number. The shopkeeper Viliam Šumichrast sold four toothbrushes at that time. On Easter Monday I had been to douse[2] his daughter Valika and she had given me a chocolate egg.

It was spring, neither too early and certainly not late; the air warmed up gradually and persistently as did the thick walls of the chilly old houses, until it finally overtook those buildings with its calm, but tireless progress up the sunny spiral. That's why I also began to slip out of the house more often. Of course winter also has a great number of attractions for boys of my age; after all, childhood and youth are nothing more than a never-ending tale written in virgin snow. It's true that, copying my parents, I too began to avoid my friends; I even played truant for a few days, but the teacher, given the exceptional circumstances, excused my absence . It seemed to me that our family was voluntarily condemning itself to a lonely and helpless future. I spent two or three days in the company of my parents and my Švošov uncle, who once more appeared unexpectedly in our house at the end of the Easter week like a silent apparition, for he said so little, at least in front of me, about what had evidently brought him over the hills to once more bang repeatedly on the bolted wooden gate to the house in which he and my mother had been born. However, I had time to notice the changes that were taking place. Nothing dramatic, in fact often hardly visible, maybe in fact unimportant: a change in the intensity and tone of my mother's voice, the purple veins that had appeared out of the blue at the root of Dad's somewhat large nose. Mother's voice, quiet and fluent not long ago, became stern, words fell from her mouth like stones from a cliff face and sometimes hesitantly, as if against her will; it was possible to glimpse in them the listlessness of unripe fruit, the anxiety of an untimely harvest and the stiffness of birds numb with cold. Yes, the weariness on my parents' faces did not escape my notice. I sometimes felt tired too, with

---

2   Easter Monday tradition in Slovakia of sprinkling or dousing women (especially single girls) to bring them health and beauty, for which men are rewarded with chocolate or painted Easter eggs, food and drink.

a fatigue that didn't seem intended for me, but for someone else; when flying over, it had been looking for a different prey and had only landed on my shoulders out of necessity. I tried to ignore it, but only managed to shake it off when I got outside our gate and then even further away, under the tree of Paradise that was reflected in the surface of the lake and opening up just like a flower. But I no longer met Betka there. As this place always reminded me of her, giving me heart-ache, I decided to wait for her in front of the school. She caught sight of me immediately, blushed and tried to pass me with her eyes fixed on the road beneath her feet. Turtle doves were cooing like mad in the branches of the walnut trees and swallows were busy collecting mud from the edges of puddles. I tapped her on the shoulder with my finger. She bent over and broke into a run. She was clearly trying to avoid me. Behind the school, propped up against the crumbling wall of the neighbouring house was her shiny, brand-new bicycle, its black lacquer glistening like asphalt after rain. The pink handles reminded me of snails. She got on it, the mudguard rattled and a moment later she was gone.

She's probably afraid I'd want to ride her bicycle, I thought bitterly. And I'd envy her it. Stuff her bike! I told myself insincerely; I even felt like shouting it so she'd hear. In those days a bicycle was a rarity. My father had been wanting to buy one for several years. After all, who wants to walk to work? If I had a bicycle, I pondered on my way home, I would go to the spa every Sunday. Not to bathe, just to stroll along the promenade. I used to go there with Mum and Dad once or twice a month to bathe. I pondered on the pool with its hot, forty-degree water, but I couldn't get Betka and her bicycle off my mind. I described my experience to Mum. She listened to me and then commented laconically: "People are afraid, that's why they avoid us." Then she told me that she had been to the rectory to see the dean. "I'm having a mass said for Tomáš. And you must stop acting as an altar boy", she announced, as if it was a condition for serving a mass for Tomáš. I couldn't understand that.

"Because they're watching us."

"Who?"

"The secret police and some people in the village."

"Me, too?"

"All of us."

At that moment the hens began clucking disparagingly in the yard. I had the feeling they were laughing at us. If I'd been outside I would certainly have flung a stone at them.

Mum was not making it up. Old Rehák came to fetch me from the school. "He's to go to the National Committee", he told the teacher.

"Can't it wait?" the teacher inquired cautiously.

"No, it can't. You know what it's about."

"He's only a child."

"I must take him. An order's an order."

On the way to the National Committee building I tried to get the municipal assistant to tell me why I'd been summoned, but he held his tongue. Instead of the committee chairman, there was a complete stranger in the office. He was probably only a few years older than Tomáš, or even the same age; tall, pale, with wavy hair, in a dark grey suit, white shirt and red tie. "Sit down," he said, pointing to a chair on the other side of the table. This was followed immediately by a question that surprised me: did I smoke? And at the same time he offered me a cigarette. Of course, I refused it. The investigator then allowed me a little time; while he browsed through some papers, I racked my brains how he could know I had tried smoking. Only Pikna and Malych could have let on about that; I used to go to the River Váh with them to catch dace. It suddenly dawned on me. Why, he's a secret policeman! He must have been asking about me at school. One of those two had grassed on me. But which? Did it matter anyway? I had very different worries just then.

Later at school I didn't say a word about my suspicions in front of Pikna and Malych. To be on the safe side I began to avoid them. Afterward several classmates avoided me as well, and not only me. An invisible sword cut hitherto solid friendships into a number of lonely communities. Everyone suffered, but no one had the courage to pick up the pieces and try to glue the broken vase back together.

The investigator put the box of cigarettes away in his pocket and smiled at me. "Your brother smokes," he remarked.

I caught his remark like a drowning man a straw. "You know our Tomáš?"

"For several years; we were pals at one time," the investigator replied. Without a smile he added that he had also graduated from the army academy.

"Are you a lieutenant too?" I exclaimed hopefully. I suddenly had the feeling that this man with a pale oval face had only come to help Tomáš.

"I've been promoted twice since that," he commented with more self-reproach than pride in his voice.

I worked out his rank in my head. Lieutenant, first lieutenant, captain. So he was a captain, I concluded. And then I reflected with disappointment on how they probably wouldn't promote Tomáš now. I looked askance at the investigator. A captain, and wearing civilian clothes! Tomáš's uniform fitted him perfectly. I remembered how I had proudly walked by his side when he was last at home. That was two years ago; it was a church festival and we went to church together, Tomáš in his officer's uniform and I in new dark blue trousers and a white shirt. People kept calling to us and we stopped; they wanted to greet Tomáš and some even shook hands with me.

Old Kováčik stopped us outside the church. He grasped Tomáš's hand for a long time, looking him up and down, as if he couldn't see enough of him. Suddenly tears came into his eyes.

"And who knows where my son is and what uniform he's wearing," he said, turning his face away.

"He'll come back. Don't lose hope."
"And maybe they'll send you there to guard him."
"Don't talk nonsense, I know what's right."
"That's good, boy. Good. Take care and God be with you."
"God be with you."

I was happy and proud; none of my classmates had such a big brother, never mind one dressed in an officer's uniform.

"Do you know where your brother is?" the captain asked.

"Yes," I replied, meekly.

"Who told you?"

I had Uncle from Švošov on the tip of my tongue, but I remembered my mother's I didn't tell them anything and I promptly found a way out: "All the village is talking about it."

"And what else are they saying"

"That there will be a trial."

"And apart from that?"

I shrugged my shoulders. "I don't know."

"Do you want to help your brother?"

"Yes," I said quietly. The dying hope in me was painfully aroused. "How?"

"By telling me everything."

"What everything?"

"Who visited you and when. Whether you've seen a gun lying around at home. What the villagers talk about among themselves. What the priest thinks about it."

"The dean?"

"The dean."

He knows I'm an altar boy. And maybe he knows Mum has had a mass said for Tomáš, I realised. My thoughts were like the swallows outside the office window. They appeared and darted away without my being able to get a grasp on them. And more and more came flying by. I realised that this secret policeman was certainly no friend of Tomáš's. If he had been, he would have brought me some message from him. "I don't know anything," I said huffily, so that it sounded the same as "I won't tell you anything".

"You're making a mistake. You certainly won't help Tomáš like that."

"If I don't know anything..." I repeated in a regretful tone.

The investigator looked at me searchingly. I felt as if his gaze was clawing at my face. I knew I must endure it. I felt every muscle in my body going tense. It was like jumping from a high tree, only I realised that it wasn't soft clay soil overgrown with even softer grass beneath me, but a stone floor. The investigator's face hardened. He got up, turned his back to me, stared out of the window and after a while muttered with unconcealed anger, "You're just as bad as your older brother. Get out of here!" He could hardly contain himself.

With no apparent haste (even though I was bursting with impatience), I backed out of the office. Then I leapt down the five steps and ran off home. In order to calm down a little, I turned off towards the lake. The alder tree was swaying in a slight breeze which did not even ruffle the surface. The shadow of the tree was swimming underwater and the sandy bottom was silent, the small stones there just gleaming every now and then like little coins. A legend came to my mind. The village was suffering from drought, the cattle were dying, the trees drying up, the potato leaves withering prematurely. People were beginning to worry about famine. At that moment, a young tramp arrived in the village. He told the inhabitants that for five gold coins he would get water for them. At that time scraping together five gold coins was no easy task. A sturdy horse could be bought for that. However, the village took up his offer. The mayor handed the money to the tramp, but the next morning they found him lying dead at the foot of Wolf Hill, without the money. However, underneath his body five springs were bubbling up. After a few weeks the clean, cool water had hollowed out a river bed in which it flows to this very day. Sometimes Betka and I would walk as far as these springs, as if we were trying to puzzle out their secret and guess what their sandy mouths were whispering, but I didn't want to go there alone. Moreover my present secret was far greater than all the others I'd ever had, though not so much for its content as for its pain. I set out for home. Mum was cross with me because I had again forgotten to bring some wood into the kitchen. And she said it was not right to be roaming about when Tomáš was in prison.

Yes, everything was clear, decided, confirmed once and for all.

The arrest of his former student did not surprise the teacher. After all, he read the newspapers, listened to the radio and so he knew what was going on in the world. How else could a lieutenant in the Czechoslovak army end up, when shortly after being made an officer he had fled over the border? "Whoever betrays the working class," he declared in front of his class, "will receive just punishment and suffer for it." Sincere disappointment and somewhat forced indignation hung in his voice like mist over the lowlands. "All those the security forces have arrested in the past few days have grievously wronged the working people, because they allowed themselves to be hired by the imperialist espionage headquarters," he declared.

I listened to him open-mouthed. It was the first time in my life I had heard of espionage headquarters. I imagined them as huge halls in which hundreds of people were sitting with headphones on their ears, trying to get connections with the whole world by means of transmitters. The teacher's voice bounced off the white walls of the classroom and fell like hail on the bare heads of the nine, ten and eleven-year-old pupils. Then the teacher explained to us why the defeated bourgeoisie had not given up and were defending their privileges by any means, including ones illegal. "These parasites lived off the calluses of your fathers. Those times are now past once and for all. It is shameful for the entire village that there were so many hostile elements in it." At that time there were already six children of class enemies attending his school. That was too much. He had begun to worry about his own livelihood. What if they should sack him from the school? What would he do? His eyes, gestures and frequent coughs betrayed his fear. He therefore concentrated on his work, taking trouble over every lesson and every pupil. After some time it seemed that everything was as it should be, but at the beginning of June, during the long break, for some reason not quite clear to the teachers, a scuffle broke out among the children, involving both boys and girls. If it hadn't been for one child's head being cut open by a stone, the teacher would not have thought the incident to be of much importance. But because of that, he was forced to deal with the matter, discover who was to blame and punish them as an example. You see, the cut head belonged to the grandson of the chairman of the National Committee. The result of the investigation did not please him, but it did surprise him. I was one of the offenders and that's why I can remember almost word for word the text of the record the teacher wrote and read out aloud to the whole class in the presence of the pupils' parents three days after the incident.

Record of the inquiry into the incident.

On June 5, 1950, during the long break, this school's fourth and fifth-year pupils were fighting among themselves. In the fight a pupil of the fourth year, Pavol Betinec, received a serious head wound. First aid was given to the pupil in question at the school and then his mother came for him and immediately took him to the district hospital for a thorough examination. In the surgical department the boy received three stitches for a laceration on his head of approximately 4 cm in length. Subsequent examination did not reveal any other harm to his health, so the pupil was sent home to be cared for there.

The investigation into the above-mentioned incident showed that the fight was between children who at the present time have a parent in prison and the children of the local functionaries of autonomous bodies and party organisations. In truth, it should be said that the incident was provoked by the pupils of the latter group, who were laughing at their classmates afflicted by the loss of one of their parents, calling them spies, criminals and enemies. Anna Slezáková caused her classmate the above-mentioned injury with an angular wooden object. Her father, Ivan Slezák, a train guard, is at the present time in custody. All those participating in the fighting will receive a worse mark for behaviour on their end-of-year school reports. Údoľany, June 6, 1950. Signed by teacher J.K.

June 6th thus became a day to remember. For me twice over. Under the paradise tree that day my eyes once more spied a little figure in a calico green and white check dress, with her back turned to me. The round fair head and perhaps even rounder little nose were lit up by the sun's rays. All the shadows disappeared from the surface of the lake. The ultramarine sky, golden sun and the leaves of the trees created a strange emerald hue in which we both wrapped ourselves as if it was a veil protecting us from the evil of the world and the approaching night. I swallowed back the reproach I had been carrying in my mouth for several weeks.

"I thought you wouldn't come."
"Why?"
"Just did."
"I saw some storks flying."
"Storks? How many were there?"
"Two. A pair. They were circling over the brick factory. I thought they were going to land, but they didn't. Did you see them?"
"No. Aren't you just making it up?"
"Have I ever told you anything that wasn't true?"
"Just wanted to be sure, because I record things like that."
"I know. That's why I'm telling you. I've heard a cuckoo as well."
"I've heard one too. I also wrote that down."

"You write everything down?"
"Everything."
"Will you let me read it some time?"
"Maybe."
"Is there anything about me there?"
"Yes."
"What?"
"That you're a good shot."
"Have you seen me?"
"Yes."
"I throw something at the tomcat every day. So he won't eat the chickens. We've got a tabby cat as well. She had kittens the day before yesterday. She's got three kittens. Pity it wasn't me who cut Betinec's head. I only hit Monček, fortunately not hard, but then I felt sorry for him, because he was cursing you the least."
"You needn't have joined in. You haven't got anyone in prison."
(Silence. All that could be heard was the lapping of the water and the cries of the swifts. I stared hard at the surface of the water. And at the toes of Betka's shoes with which she was scattering a molehill.) After a while she said, "I must be going. Mum asked me not to hang around."
"Does she know you're here?"
"No. Dad doesn't want us to meet. It could put him in a bad light. He works in the district offices, you know that."
"I know."
"Well, I'll be off."
"I must go too."
"Let's run."
(The water sighed regretfully. It loved to hear children talking. From now on it would melancholically repeat a few of the syllables it remembered. The grass stood on tiptoe and stared at the departing pair. A cuckoo called. In the forest above the village the next day's white mist was gathering.)

Time is cosmic wind. Although it has enough space for its wings, it is fondest of quiet nooks. This is fatal for many people for whom every second of life seems like a stone in their shoe. For them any journey will lead through a vale of tears. They will see its infinity as an infinity of pain. For the most part these feelings are justified. At night only light can be seen. Wind blows out candles.

Although I tried to see and find out more than was allowed for my size and age (measured more by heartbeats than data in the registry office), I was still the last to learn the latest events concerning Tomáš. Perhaps that was why I had too little time to persuade my father by begging or sulking to let me attend the trial. Dad received a summons to the court hearing. The invitation was for two members of the family. The hearing was not open to the public and it was to last three days, but the summons was only valid for one day, the last one, which was when the sentence would be pronounced. Mum relinquished her right in favour of her brother and so in the end it was my uncle who travelled with Dad to Bratislava. He had been to see Tomáš's defence lawyer in advance; Mum sent him goose fat, thinking he would defend Tomáš better.

On the day I was a terrible nuisance. I was cantankerous, I refused to do as I was told, and I was objectionable to my mother and to myself. It was the thirtieth of June, the day school reports are handed out. Mum hardly managed to get me ready for school. The only remark that helped her was: "Tomáš would be cross if you didn't go." At that instant the obstinate ram became a humble lamb. I arrived late. The teacher acted as if my lateness came as no surprise. (That day two boys and one girl were absent from school.) He probably realised I would bear any kind of punishment with proud indifference.

That day I came to know the sandy essence of time. My mouth and eyes were full of it and everywhere I was aware of its unbearable presence, reminiscent of eternity.

Dad and Uncle returned in the early hours of the morning. I awoke to a tapping on the window. Mum had locked the kitchen door. Half asleep, I groped my way to the door and turned the key in the lock. The sun was just beginning to scramble up into the sky. Dad and Uncle stepped into the kitchen. Mum stood motionless in the doorway to the room. In an instant I was wide awake. The calm and warmth of sleep were suddenly transformed into the sharp, cold edge of reality. No one uttered a word. Dad went to lie down without eating anything. And my Švošov uncle seemed reluctant to reveal the truth. Mum offered him a dram of plum brandy and sliced two sausages on a cutting board and put some bread on the table. Uncle ate without saying a word. He cut a slice of bread into all sorts of triangles and rectangles; he stuck his knife into the pieces of sausage and put them into his mouth with a kind of insufferable dignity. I didn't understand why he wasn't saying anything. And why Mum didn't ask anything. Wasn't she curious to know how the trial had gone? I was confused. I decided to wait. When Uncle had finished eating I would ask him outright. I was burning with impatience. If I had been in my uncle's shoes, I would already have poured out everything I had seen, heard, undergone. He just chewed and chewed. It took him ages to finish eating. If only he would choke! At that moment a thought occurred to me: Dad would be sure to tell me! I didn't even have time to grasp the handle of the door to the room when Uncle stopped me. "Leave your Dad alone. He's in a very bad way. On the journey back I was afraid he wouldn't make it and I would have to leave him in hospital in some other town."

I felt ashamed of my impatience and fixed my helpless gaze on Mum. Why didn't she at least urge Uncle to say at last how they had got on in Bratislava? She sat down next to me and I heard her breathe in deeply and hold her breath, and only then did I notice that she had on a black dress, the one she had worn to Grandma's funeral the year before last. When I saw her so quiet and black, a floodgate opened inside me and tears filled my eyes. Mum took me in her arms like a little child and I sobbed and sniffled there and to the accompaniment of my muffled lament, Uncle considerately and unhurriedly recounted in detail what had happened. I stopped crying and hung on his words like a bunch of grapes on a vine. I would have torn the words from his throat if I could, because it was clear that Uncle was reluctant to say what he would anyway have to say in the end. For incomprehensible, perhaps almost uncanny reasons, in this story he had been entrusted with the role of messenger. Tomáš had been sentenced to death! Old Kováčik, the former mayor, to twenty-five years in prison and expulsion from the district for ever. The others had received lighter sentences.

At that moment I stopped breathing. Perhaps I wanted to die. And thus spare myself Uncle's long, too long account, that like smooth water under immense pressure changed into splinters of glass, falling into the roaring waterfall of awareness. I now knew what a chalice of bitterness tasted like. And I also noticed that my mother's eyes remained dry. I couldn't know that she had wept away all her tears in the previous nights.

"I guessed how it would turn out," she said several minutes later. "I dreamed that our Tomáš was getting married and I was sitting beside him at the table instead of the bride."

In my diary beside the date July 1, 1950 you can find this note: "Tomáš has been sentenced to death. But he won't die. I shall free him."

I was eleven years old when my brother was sentenced to death. And five other children were deprived of their fathers for many years. For children of our age this was an incomprehensible occurrence, a mystery only intensified by the reticence of the adults. In my mind imprisonment was associated with crime and deserved punishment. There was no one in the village with the necessary experience in this regard. Not even the oldest inhabitants could remember someone from the village being put in jail. We children didn't understand anything, the adults likewise, but at least they had the opportunity to draw on various sources of information—although they only made them feel even more insecure. In public they began to behave timidly; they were fearful and suspicious, while after some time their children might seem to a chance observer to be spectators or listeners not personally involved in the story. No one reproached us for this, however; rather the contrary—my parents and the mothers of the other children comforted themselves with the thought that at least their children were not fretting over what had happened to their husbands and sons. This was poor comfort, it's true, but in the situation in which they found themselves it was a useful substitute for real consolations, which for some reason were late to arrive and were hiding somewhere just as treasure hides from human eyes in the ground and swallows arrive late.

The sun that rose that day seemed to have no intention of setting. It burned in the sky like a torch and no sooner had it disappeared behind the hills than it immediately lit them again with its hot breath like a wisp of threshed barley straw. For six or maybe even seven weeks an unprecedented heatwave tormented the people, animals and grass and no house or even shade provided sufficient shelter from it; the water in the streams and rivers warmed up rapidly, as if the Earth's core had immodestly bared itself before an audience of drunkards and inhabitants of hell. The wind reeked of desert sand and drove before it little stalks of devastated crops. Sometimes mirages of nearby oases offered water to thirsty herds. Imagine eleven-year olds, and even younger children, boys and girls, standing on the banks of a stream and searching the water for answers to questions that even adults did not dare ask themselves.

For these children the summer was a painful stubble field they had no choice but to walk through until sunset. The sun, however, was in no hurry to set and night seemed no longer to exist. The village was dying. But I stayed awake; once more alone under the alder I concocted brave plans. Packs of wild beasts hung around my soul. I did not want to be a child. I wanted my innocence to stop protecting me; I no longer even wished for the help of a guardian angel. It's true, I would pray "Guardian angel, watch over my little soul," but it was only my mouth that prayed. My heart was ablaze like a burning haystack. No one suspected that I was shedding the snake skin of childhood. Only the aged dean noticed the change coming over me. One evening he came to visit us at home, because father, who had been in bed with pneumonia ever since that fateful day, had taken a turn for the worse. "Dear child," he said to me softly. "Don't you want to make confession too?"

I shook my head. At that moment I was carrying only one sin on my soul: not even the idea that my father was dying filled my heart with natural sorrow. Not that I didn't think about death at all. In fact I thought about it more often than about life. But I didn't want to talk about it. Because of Tomáš. I was afraid that somehow my thoughts might bring it closer to him. Did he really have to die?

"The High Court will decide everything," said the Archangel—my Švošov uncle.

Time is the tightly-closed mouth of eternity. On occasion people imitate its secrecy, although the most difficult thing for children is to say nothing and to refrain from play.

What do you expect to hear from an eleven-year-old boy who shouldn't even be thinking about certain things, never mind talking about them, especially when questioned by adults? He'd rather tell you about the emerald green grasshoppers with transparent wings which were to be seen in swarms that summer when raking the stubble of oat and barley fields. And he might also place the little stone of his secret on the scales of your conscience, because it was hurting him and weighing him down more than the great secrets of adults do. It is a good thing the sun did not scorch him that summer as it did the harvests the farmers wanted to boast of not only to people, but also to God.

But let's walk on through the stubble fields. We may be able to wash our bleeding feet soon in a clear stream. The alder rustled in the dry summer wind like the sails of God's mill. Betka went to stay with her grandmother in Chynorany. She would be there until the end of the school holidays. Dad gradually got better. Towards evening he would go and sit on the bench in front of the house, always smoking half a packet of cigarettes, even though the doctor had strictly forbidden him to smoke. On that bench my next sin was born: it seemed to me that my father's recovery lessened the chances of saving Tomáš's life. Of course this was nonsense, but I was just examining every possibility that could help my brother's plight. Some time at the end of August Dad got worse again and the very same day a letter arrived from Tomáš. Mum opened the envelope. She began to read it aloud, but after the first sentence she got a lump in her throat and could not continue. She passed the letter to me. I recognised my brother's small, rounded writing. How many lines was it? Twenty? Thirty? And such ordinary sentences that said nothing. I, at least, had expected more detailed news.

Dear Parents and Brother,
How long it is since we last saw each other! And how much has happened in the past few months. My life and no doubt yours too have changed unrecognisably. I think of you every day and it pains me to think that I have caused you so much distress. I have put myself completely in the hands of Divine justice. Ján, I urgently beg you to be considerate and kind to Mum and Dad. Life is so hard for them; at least you should not trouble them, when I have given them so much worry. The address will have told you that I have been moved from Bratislava to Leopoldov. At least I'm with other people. They've told me we will have our appeal trial in Prague on the third of September. I would be glad if someone from the family could come. At least our Švošov uncle, as he has a railway employee's pass. Don't be afraid for me. I know and firmly believe that the Lord of life and death decides everything. With a sincere kiss, Your Tomáš.

An appeal trial! I immediately grasped the opportunity.

"I'll go," I cried. "Send me to Prague."

My mother didn't seem to hear me. She was standing at the window and looking out, perhaps at the yard, maybe further, at the foothills laid waste by the hot weather, or at Tomáš's future. She saw the outlines of this in dreams which she did not talk about to anyone right up to her death. Dad, ailing and weakened by illness, sat dumbly on a chair, his right hand absent-mindedly crumbling a cigarette he did not dare put in his mouth in front of Mum. He suddenly began coughing, as if choking on a tear, and it was clear he was suffocating.

"Medicine, where's my medicine?" he wheezed for help. Mum shook a white tablet out of a little dark round bottle. She ran water into a white cup with a broken-off handle and handed it to Dad. Dad impatiently drank down the medicine, spilling water over his shirt and trousers. Even at such a moment I wasted no time. "I want to visit Tomáško. I want to see him. This time I'll go. Nobody else," I repeated obstinately, because I was afraid of being too late with my request. "Mummy, say I can go, please!" I urged.

"I shall go with your uncle," Mum said calmly, as if she had already anticipated this moment and had planned every step.

"I want to go with you. I must."

"Trains are expensive."

"I only need a half fare."

"Only two members of the family can go to the court. You will stay home with Dad. Someone must look after the poultry," my mother decided pitilessly and with finality. The tone in which she said it indicated that there was no point in pressing the matter any further. I began howling like a little child and tears came to my eyes: "But I must speak to him!"

"You don't have to," my mother rebuffed me wearily, stroking my head. I angrily jerked my head away in order to shake off her caress then ran out into the yard and off to the lake. There I sobbed until the evening. My parents knew nothing about my plan to free Tomáš from prison. I had formed it only a short time before.

One whole day I had helped the Kováčik family with their threshing. During the lunch break Kováčik's seventeen-year-old grandson Martin, who had been expelled from grammar school because of his grandfather and who was now training to be a tinsmith, pulled a smallish object wrapped in brown wax paper from under the thresher behind the barn, in the middle of the circle trampled by the hooves of Kováčik's horse. When he unwrapped it, a gun lay in his palm. A real, black shiny revolver. He handed it to me to feel its weight. More than its pressure, I felt its coldness and smoothness. My heart started beating wildly.

"A revolver! Is it loaded?" I asked him in a whisper. "Of course." He took out the magazine, pressed one bullet out of it and handed it to me. I cautiously took it between my fingers and immediately returned it to him. I was shaking all over from excitement and fear. I didn't even dare to ask him where he got the gun and ammunition from. He adroitly pushed the bullet back into the magazine. I realised it was not the first time he had done that. He weighed the revolver in his hand. "With this we could get them all out from there, what do you say?" He looked at me as if he were only waiting for me to agree. "I read a novel about a travelling salesman wrongly sentenced to death who saved his life like this," he added in order to be sure to win me over for his plan.

I could easily imagine Tomáš with a gun in his hand. After all, he was a soldier, an officer. But Martin? However, I couldn't get the idea out of my head. First I would have to think up a way of smuggling the revolver into the prison. The visit! I had to go to see him! My parents had to take me to Prague. I only had to hint what it was about and Tomáš would be certain to come up with something. My mind was blank, but thoughts were already beginning to be scattered around it by an invisible wind, like bits of straw in a stubble field. I would tell him: I have a present with me that you will like very much. I hoped he would understand what I was hinting at. After all, he was brave and he was a soldier.

Martin wrapped the gun up in the paper and returned it to its hiding place. Then he looked at me gravely.

"Swear you'll not mention that gun to anyone!"

"I swear," I muttered, my throat tight.

We went back to the threshing. Martin passed the sheaves to the feeder and I carried the threshed straw away on a pitchfork to the stack beside the barn. It was the middle of August. There was a wind blowing and it scattered pieces of straw over the backyards. Within me, however, there was a gale raging.

I had to do something.

That evening, at night in fact, under cover of darkness, I slipped out of the house. I wanted to steal that gun and save Tomáš. But it was no longer in the same hiding place. So that was that. My oath condemned me to silence. And I couldn't go to Martin; I would have had to confess I'd wanted to steal it.

The next day I had to force myself to write a letter to Tomáš. I could only manage a couple of sentences.

"It's the school holidays. Pity you aren't at home. Write more often. Don't worry about me. I greet you a hundred times."

I don't know why, but I liked that "hundred times". Later, though, when Mum took the letter to Angela Kováčiková to put in the post box in town, it began to seem inappropriate to me, even brash. I resolved that the words "a hundred times" would not appear in my next letter. Then it occurred to me that I would not be writing very soon, because in the heading above Tomáš's letter there was written in black and white: A prisoner in the 1st category of privileges may send and receive letters once every 2 weeks, in the 2nd once every 3 weeks, in the 3rd once every 4 weeks, in the 4th once every 5 weeks and in the 5th once every 6 weeks. At the same intervals they may receive visits on Tuesdays, Thursdays, Saturdays and Sundays.

Now I felt like a prisoner myself. Like a bird in a cage. It stretches its wings in vain; it cannot fly out. It was ten more days before Mum and Uncle were to go to Prague for the hearing. My whole being focused on that day alone. The general tension was eased a little by the news from the Bratislava lawyer, addressed to my Švošov uncle: "The matter is going well. There is no direct aggravating circumstance in this client's case. On the contrary, in mitigation is the fact that although he had a weapon on him when he was arrested, he clearly had no intention of using it." One night shortly after this, someone wrote in whitewash on the wall of the fire station in large letters: COMMUNIST MURDERERS. People hardly had time to read it before the secret police appeared in the village. The investigations did not exclude me. This time it was a one-armed fifty-year old who took me to task.

"I lost this arm fighting against fascism. Can you see it?" he lifted his stump above the table.

"Yes, I can," I mumbled resignedly.

"Do you know what fascism was?"

"Yes. Germans," I promptly replied.

"And what are you?"

"A Slovak."

"You're not a Slovak," the investigator contradicted. "There are no Slovaks in this village. They're all fascists."

"There aren't any fascists here," I declared, defending the honour of the whole village.

"There are!" yelled the man, his round face turning red. "Who else but a fascist could write something as outrageous as what we found written on the walls of the fire station?" It was a rhetorical question. The investigator fixed me with a stare. "It's obvious it wasn't you," he said after a while, maybe to reassure me and at the same time to win me over a little. "But no doubt you know who it was," he attacked out of the blue, without taking his eyes off me.

"I don't know. I don't know anything about it," I cried. I very nearly blurted out that the whole of our family condemned the unknown perpetrator for his foolhardiness, which was how we saw the inscription on the fire station. After all, it could snuff out that little spark of hope referred to by Tomáš's lawyer! "I don't know anything about it. Nor do my parents. No one knows," I spluttered quickly and hardly comprehensibly and my face must have shown so much sincerity and helplessness that the investigator believed me and let me go. The police did not manage to discover the perpetrator, never mind punish him, in spite of the fact that they interrogated about half the inhabitants of the village.

At long last the thunder and rain arrived. First just a few drops and then some time after midnight there was a real downpour. Streams of muddy water rushed down the village. However, by morning the sky had cleared and the sun took the land and people into its warm embrace.

People didn't know what to think of it. Not everyone had managed to get the harvest in from the fields and thresh the grain, so now they were in a hurry to make up for it. On account of the mud they had to leave the wagons a long way from the stacked sheaves and so they carried the sheaves to them on their backs. The thresher clattered noisily long into the night. The threshing took twice as long as in other years. The damp grain had to be dried as well, by turning it over with shovels sometimes twice a day.

It was while we were hurriedly catching up with the summer chores that the day of Tomáško's appeal trial arrived. Mum and my uncle from Švošov set out a day earlier, late Monday afternoon, leaving me at home with my sick father. I put a cup of linden tea on a chair next to Dad's bed. Before that, I carried out the chamber pot, wiped up the puddle under the bed and I was about to leave, when Dad called to me: "Stay here! Don't leave me alone."

His eyes were sunken in his head, reminding me of wells. His yellow complexion had become a mask of dried mud. Suddenly I had a feeling someone had come in. Tomáš. He stood in the middle of the room, the floor creaked, he looked at us in surprise, but as if we were strangers, as if he were asking who we were and what we were doing there, and then he left.

No, no. It was not like that. His image must have been formed by the tears that had come to our eyes out of the blue. Dad turned to face the wall and I tiptoed out into the yard and sat on the bench under the window. I sat there, I suppose without moving, until sunset. The apparition came back to me. I could talk to it, but I got no answer to my questions. My brother and I had an endless night and a terribly long day ahead of us. I slept in my mother's bed in case my father took a turn for the worse. In that case I was to run to the dean and ask him to telephone to the town for a doctor. Fortunately this wasn't necessary. The dawn always brings hope. The birds announced themselves early and the dew lit up the grass with a silvery sheen. The day warmed itself in the sunshine like a lizard on a rock. But it dragged on interminably. Mum only returned home from Prague towards evening and alone; Uncle had remained there to explore the chances of finding somebody who would intervene for Tomáš in the President's office. The High Court had confirmed the Bratislava court's verdict. Mum sat beside Dad's bed. "They're going to kill him ... But why, for God's sake, why?" she kept repeating monotonously. But she did not weep. Dad was silent for a long time and when he spoke, his voice was as thin as a spider's thread.

"Did they allow you to visit him?"

Mum nodded.

"How long did they leave you together?"

"Ten minutes."

From what she said, I understood they had seen Tomáš and spoken to him through a thick steel mesh. My plan to free him was impossible. So there was no help for Tomáš. "He would die! Die! He would die!" echoed in my head like in an empty church, when the sacristan snuffs out the candles on the altar.

There was nothing we could do now. There was no point in planning anything else. I hadn't met Martin again since the threshing. And I didn't look for him either. That day of the last hearing neither Dad nor I had eaten a crumb. Food had not even entered our heads. Mum spread butter on a slice of bread and handed it to me without a word. She took another to Dad.

But the next day one spark of hope did flare up in me after all. A conjuror appeared in the village. Mum gave me some money to go and see the performance. As it was a warm evening, the show took place in the school playground. The last item on the programme caught my attention in particular. The conjuror's assistant handcuffed the conjuror and tied him up with rope, locked him up in a wooden box, winding chains round it, which she secured with about six padlocks. Then she covered the box for a few seconds with a red sheet and a moment later the conjuror emerged from behind the curtain without handcuffs and ropes, as free as a bird. And the box hadn't been opened at all. This man could free our Tomáš from prison! I thought excitedly. An hour after the performance had finished, I timidly knocked on the door of the conjuror's caravan. The door opened and a tousled female head appeared round it.

"What do you want?" she asked grumpily.

"To talk to your....master," I didn't know what to call the conjuror. Later it occurred to me—Master Conjuror.

"He's asleep. He's very tired."

"But I must speak to him," I said tearfully.

She stepped outside, closing the door behind her. She put her arm round my shoulders and we went down the steps like this. "You've run away from home, haven't you? You want to become a conjuror?" she probed gently. There was so much sadness in her voice that I was quite overcome and I told her what I wanted—to ask whether the master conjuror could free our Tomáš from prison and thus save his life.

"You dear little donkey," she whispered, ruffling my hair. Tears could be heard in her voice. "That wasn't real. It's just a trick. An illusion. That wouldn't help your brother. Besides, he is closely guarded in his cell. They won't let anyone in to see him and certainly not some conjuror. I know how it is. My father has already been in prison for three years and he has another ten to go. And I can't help him."

"But they want to kill my brother!" I cried and immediately broke off, shrinking to the size of a pygmy, even though no one could hear, apart from the stars twinkling in the vast, clear September sky. At that same moment several of them fell from the fingers of the blue darkness into the transparent shirt of the approaching night.

"Go to bed. Don't think about it anymore. It's madness." It was not madness, but just a match with which I wanted to light my way along the paths of life.

At this point the right thing to do might be to hurry up and proclaim the end of the story. But the clock of time does not cease to tick; the movement of the hands is inexorably approaching the last hour when the story must reach its climax. Strange: this time it was me who received the decision of the High Court confirming my brother's death sentence as if it were the irrevocable will of life. My parents, my Švošov uncle, even the chairman of the local National Committee in the name of the inhabitants of the municipality wrote to the President pleading for a pardon. However, on a number of occasions I caught myself thinking of him as already dead. And in my mind I talked to him as if he were dead. No doubt his last letter was to blame for this. He was back in Leopoldov prison again. "Not the courts, but the Lord of life and death decides about human existence or non-existence. Ján, be good to our parents; make up for the grief I have caused them with the joy they will one day have from you." Once again it was my task to reply. But this time it was not just a worry; it was heart-breaking. What should I write him? What can interest a person condemned to death? And so I wrote that I'd begun to attend the secondary school, that I was saving up for a bicycle, because

I didn't want to walk there on foot, and that there was a terrible gale on Our Lady's Day which toppled trees and tore off barn roofs.

Could this information interest someone who, though still alive, was in fact already dead? Permission came for a visit and I accepted the chance to see my brother with an indifferent heart. I went there just with Mum, even though Dad was feeling better.

I saw this invincible stone fortress, the heavy gate, towers, soldiers and weapons. And a stranger who fortunately recognised me at once and spoke to me.

"Shrimp! My, how you've grown!"

I did not know what to say. "I'm almost twelve," I boasted.

"Was the water in the Váh warm?"

"As tea." I tried to force a smile, but without much success. The visit was very short. Mum reserved a minute or two for herself. "I've brought you a few apples. Summer ones."

And meanwhile I searched for memories, dipping for them into the waters of a thousand seas.

Look, Shrimp! A pike! Where?

There. There. In the shade, under that alder.

I thought it was a branch.

Pikes are cunning. They pretend they're not doing anything and as soon as they get the chance, they attack.

(White clouds float on the surface, making the water seem deeper and cleaner than it really is. The pike stares at me. But when I look again, the pike is no longer there.)

Where is it? Where did it go?

It escaped when you moved. It's a shy fish. Are predatory fish afraid too?

They're not afraid; they just don't trust anyone.

(A scarcely audible splash and an arrow-like ripple on the water's surface betray the attack of a muskrat. It leaves its burrow under the right bank for shelter on the left side. The muskrat gives me a feeling of repulsion and fear.)

How did muskrats get here? They've sprung up from underground, or what?

They've swum here from the River Váh.

I'm scared.

What of, Shrimp? After all, I'm here!

(The images disappear and once more leap around on the surface. Dragonflies flit among them.)

In that prison I wanted, with the help of my brother, to discover and understand the meaning of everything that was washing over me and re-creating me, as if I had now, at the age of twelve, been born again, but without that very necessary crying and bawling with which I would announce to all my new arrival in the world.

The plums and pears grew ripe; it was time to pick them; the walnuts began to open... We did all these jobs without thinking. It was something like long-lasting unconsciousness, apathy of body and soul, cataleptic stiffness that almost transformed us into dummies in the great shop window of life. The whole of this time I didn't go even once to the lake and Betka passed me without a word on her bicycle to and from school. The families of the other prisoners also began to behave in a more relaxed and self-confident manner. They didn't have anyone sentenced to death. We could soon run into them in the street or in Šumichrast's shop with smiles on their faces and sparks of joy in their eyes; they had detached themselves from our sad procession once and for all, leaving just a handful of us in it—my parents, my Švošov uncle and me.

However, one day in October an unexpected event brightened up this gloomy autumn scene. When lessons were over, I caught sight of Betka in front of the old school building. I didn't suppose she was waiting for me; after all, not only was her father a district functionary, but her mother had been appointed Secretary to the National Committee in the neighbouring village. Our meeting could endanger Betka's parents and I did not want to have this on my conscience. Betka simply stood in my way, thus forcing me to stop and look at her. As we were not in the same class, it was only now I could take a close look at her. She had grown noticeably; she was even a centimetre or two taller than me. She had returned from her grandmother's rounder and suntanned and later she told me that she had spent part of the holidays with her Chynorany grandfather and grandmother in Miškolc in the house of her grandfather's brother. My eyes not only fell on her plump tanned legs, but on her full lips and distinctly budding breasts under her calico dress and angora pullover. I felt the blood rushing to my face. I didn't hear what she was saying to me. I only saw her moving lips and heard the pounding of my own heart. I was standing before a mysterious cave. From those moving lips an unknown visitor was trying to enter my home; the current of a swollen river was pressing against the walls of the flimsy little house of my imagination and there was a danger that it would soon collapse. Fortunately, through the roar of that water, I heard Betka's surprised question.

"Ján! Are you listening to me at all?" I nodded. "Then come on," she said, taking me by the hand.

It was time to come to my senses and wake up from my dream. "Where are you taking me?" I demurred.

She looked at me and giggled. She realised I had not been listening to her. She may have noticed the embarrassment that my evasive eyes could not hide. I was standing naked before her and she had the opportunity to laugh at me, or clothe me in the spider silk of her own innocence. She chose the latter possibility.

"I asked you to come to the cake shop. It's my birthday tomorrow. Are you coming or not?" she asked impatiently. However, I heard tenderness and uneasiness in her voice.

In T., apart from the secondary school, there was also a cinema, a cake shop and a railway station at which even the express trains stopped on account of the spa. The words "cake shop" restored my confused, scattered awareness. Sweet things can help a person to come to terms with unhappiness and with him or herself even in adulthood. We sat in the dim light of what had once been Kohn's cake shop. Kohn, the owner of both the cake shop and the bakery, had not returned from the concentration camp after the war. We sat in the shop and Betka ordered choux pastry rings, slices of punch cake and raspberry lemonade; we chatted about trivialities and kept giggling over everything. We were children once again. There were only the two of us in the whole world.

"Grandad lost his way in Miškolc. We thought we'd never see him again and then he appeared just before midnight. And do you know what he told Grandma when she asked where he'd been so long?"

"What?"

"That he'd been home. He said he'd left his pipe in Chynorany and as he couldn't be without it, he'd popped out for it. And he immediately puffed at this pipe in front of Grandma. And it's about six hundred kilometres from Miškolc to Chynorany. When Grandma pressed him, he confessed that he had got lost."

We transformed ordinary holiday episodes into miraculous events; the sugar went to our heads like wine and evidently all this (though unforced) amusement had one purpose: it was a farewell celebration; our childhood wanted to part with us in a dignified and unforgettable manner. Thus for a while I was able to forget Tomáš, Dad and Mum, the world in general. We were laughing and instead of words we were reiterating our childhood's fragile happiness. But when we emerged from the overheated cake shop, the sharp whip of the October wind lashed our faces, huge grey-black clouds chased over our heads and the chilly embrace of premature twilight wrapped itself around us. We both suddenly fell silent, perhaps frightened by the natural elements, none of which boded well. I realised that because of the cake shop, Betka had

walked to school that day instead of going by bike. Scared and chilled, we ran the whole way home. And our parting was brief: "Take care, Ján."
"You take care too."
Those were the last gifts of that autumn.

On November 9th, during a history lesson, the headmaster came into our class. He was a tall, middle-aged man and his eternal frown scared us. We all sprang to our feet and old Mrs Rolincová, our teacher, hurried surprisingly swiftly to meet him, a smile on her face. The headmaster bent towards her and whispered something in her ear. I noticed that she turned pale, looked at me and said in a hoarse voice, "Ján, take your things and run off home. You are to hurry and not stop anywhere on the way." It must have been about two in the afternoon when I came dashing in. I had to change quickly and eat. Mum and my Švošov uncle were in a hurry; they only told me that we were going to visit Tomáš; apparently there had been a call from Bratislava to the National Committee that we had been allowed a visit and that we must report to the Palace of Justice by midnight at the latest. Uncle had managed to buy tickets on the Slovak Arrow, a blue express train, and we simply mustn't miss it, because it was the last train to Bratislava. Strange: I didn't think of Dad all this time; after all, Mum didn't even peep into the room where he was lying, as if she wanted to protect him from our nervous haste. I only became aware of his existence when Aurea, Kováčik's daughter arrived at our house. She was a nun of a forbidden order and they didn't want to employ her in the hospital even though she was a nurse. She would look after Dad in our absence. I realised that I was going to Bratislava in his place. But just before we left the house, the bedroom door opened and there, clearly summoning up all his strength, stood Dad. He gazed at my mother with a look I had never seen before or since in human eyes. We all fell silent, immobilised within and without. Dad's mouth opened, but the time that passed between that beginning and the utterance of the first word was as long as that needed for the creation of the world.

"Tell him... tell... tell..." He spoke weakly, visibly shaking all over, "may... may... Ah, no, nothing!" he suddenly cried out, his eyes filling with tears. He abruptly turned round and slammed the door behind him. The bed creaked as he collapsed onto it and then a sob was heard that seemed to cut into the wall like a knife and quivered and echoed in each of us separately.

Abraham had come to terms with the sacrifice of his son Isaac.

Mum moved towards the door to the room, but Angela Kováčiková, the nun and nurse, held her back. "Go in peace. I'll take care of him," she said, perhaps even too calmly. Mum's eyes fell on the clock and she nodded helplessly.

"It's high time we got a move on," said Uncle. Mum threw a woollen shawl over her black suit, Uncle put on his railwayman's winter coat and I donned a grey fleece coat with worn sleeves. Then Mum handed me a shapeless parcel, tied up with string. Considering its size, it was surprisingly light. At four o'clock we at last left the house. The express departed at half past five. The walk to the station took just under an hour. It was getting dark. A flock of crows was hovering over the fields and then flew off towards the hills. White frost was glittering on the trees, a reminder that winter was not far off.

At first the journey by train seemed like an undeserved treat. For me the train was an incredibly beautiful mystery. While Mum and Uncle were silent for most of the journey, I kept up a lively commentary on everything I saw through the train window. It was the first time in my life I had travelled in an express train like this. In the dim light the quiet, deserted little stations the train flew through made me think of enchanted castles. The big stations, on the other hand, filled me with wonder and curiosity. Where could so many people be going? Where did they come from? On occasion, the express stopped in the middle of black fields lit only by moonlight. Snow clouds rolled across the sky and the full moon crept among them like a hungry wolf. My reserves of energy were gradually spent; somewhere after Leopoldov they were completely exhausted and I slept through the remainder of the journey. I woke to the rattle and jolting of the carriages and the clatter of the buffers.

"Wake up. We're in Bratislava. Put your coat on," I heard my mother say. The clock on the platform showed half past ten. Snow could be felt in the air. The dinging of a tram could be heard somewhere nearby. Nevertheless, we went on foot from the station. After about forty minutes we stopped in front of a big, tall building.

I read the inscription above the entrance: "The Palace of Justice". Why palace? I wondered. Could it be the residence of some king? I stopped looking for the answer, because I suddenly realised that I would very soon be seeing Tomáš. My heart began to beat suffocatingly. I took such a deep breath of sharp air that I began coughing. "It's nothing," I assured my mother when she looked at me in alarm. I was a tense bow string. The arrow could fly out at any moment; it pressed against my chest and was aimed directly at my heart. I felt that moment was near. Then there would be one twelve-year-old heart less in the world.

We came to a halt in front of the large door. The curiosity normal in a boy of my age helped me to overcome the dread that gripped me. So, they were keeping our Tomáš behind these strong, heavy doors, I thought. The guard on duty was sitting in a sentry box. Uncle handed him his and Mum's identity cards. The guard first looked at me.

"How old are you?" "Twelve," I whispered.

"He... that one... he's what to him?" he turned to Mum.

"Brother. His younger brother."

The guard laid aside our identity cards and jotted something down in a notebook. Then he telephoned somewhere. It all took ages. Finally the large door opened. We immediately found ourselves in front of another door and another check point. The officer (he turned out to be the head of the prison guard) and another woman officer searched us thoroughly and checked Uncle and Mum's bags.

The woman officer felt the parcel. "What's in this?" "Clothes for my son," Mum said quietly.

"Leave them here for the moment and I'll give you them when you leave the building. Now you'll go with the Chief Officer. He'll take you to the visiting room." She put the parcel away in a green metal cupboard. I noticed that she did not lock it.

The Chief Officer led us through a labyrinth of short and long corridors. Through the barred windows we could see a courtyard lit up by floodlights and surrounded by buildings with similarly barred, but smaller windows. The lift (another first for me) took us to the first floor. A moment later we found ourselves in a room without windows, but with two doors. The door we came through was guarded by two prison officers armed with machine guns. One of them shut the door behind us when we were inside.

This was the visiting room. It was divided in two by a long, wide table and a high metal mesh, which seemed to grow up from its middle. There were chairs at the table; three on our side, just one opposite.

"Sit down and wait," the Chief Officer said.

The door on the opposite side was painted green. After a while two officers came through it almost soundlessly. They took up positions in the corners of the room. Then Tomáš appeared in the doorway, followed by a third officer, who was a pleasant-looking woman of about thirty. I can't remember anything more of what she looked like, because from that moment on my eyes were fixed on Tomáš. I could barely recognise him. He had lost weight and was incredibly pale, as if whitewashed. The metal mesh was dense, so we couldn't shake hands, only press them to the mesh. Tears were glistening in Mum's eyes, but she did not begin crying. I felt the touch of Tomáš's palm on mine. It was cold and damp. It only lasted a brief moment, however, and this lessened my torment a little. I was in the grip of an emotion that I cannot define even now. Curiosity, that helper of little children, which had until now held my hand, deserted me. Instead horror, awe and fear remained. That feeling paralysed me and stuck in my throat like an enormous bone; it was as heavy as a stone in my stomach, but its invisible, though sensed presence suggested death. In the meantime, while this whirlpool of anxiety dragged me into its centre, Tomáš greeted Uncle and then took a packet of cigarettes from the pocket of his strange rough prison uniform and looked timidly at the woman officer standing at the head of the table to see whether she would allow him to light up. She smiled and nodded understandingly. He hurriedly put a cigarette in his mouth, struck a match and hunching his head between his shoulders, as if he were standing in a draught, he lit the cigarette. Then he eagerly drew the smoke into his lungs, half-closed his eyes blissfully and then opened them again, glancing at us in wonder, as if he had seen and recognised us only now. He smiled guiltily, like a boy caught smoking.

"I smoke a lot," he said quietly.

"You do that," Uncle said encouragingly.

"These are my last," he tapped the box.

"I'll leave you mine." Uncle pulled a crumpled box of broken cigarettes out of the pocket of his heavy railwayman's fur coat and put them on the table before him.

"I can't take them without permission," said Tomáš.

Uncle looked helplessly at the woman officer. She walked towards him unhurriedly. With her eyes she gave a sign to the guard standing behind us.

"Let me," he took the packet of cigarettes and checked the contents. "It's okay," he said. "We'll give them to the prisoner after the visit."

Mum also took advantage of the opportunity. From her bag she drew out a jar of acacia honey, a couple of thick-skinned apples and put them on the table. One apple rolled towards Tomáš. "Give him this too,

please." The woman officer shrugged her shoulders, looking awkward.
"It's up to the prisoner," she said indecisively.
"Keep it, Mum," Tomáš said.
"Honey's good for the nerves," she objected timidly.
"Please, Mum," Tomáš said despairingly.
"Don't press it on him, you can see he doesn't need anything," Uncle intervened at the last moment. It really was the last, because Tomáš's calm was at the end of its tether. He lit another cigarette and then chain smoked, lighting one cigarette from the previous one. In the meantime he asked Mum about Dad's health, me about school, Uncle about his work and then the conversation began to dry up. Surprisingly, it was Tomáš who thought up something first.
"What about snow? Did Martin arrive on a white horse?"[3]
"No, he didn't," Uncle replied sadly.
"At least you won't use up so much wood."
"We've got enough of that, maybe even for two winters," Mum joined in the conversation. "Dad receives wood from the Forestry Office."
"Since they installed electricity we've not needed so much," Uncle remarked.
I was the only one not to join in the conversation. All my thoughts deserted me, no word pressed itself on my tongue, my memory called up recollections and images from its deepest depths and then these flew over the landscape of my mind at a dizzying speed. I would have liked it to change into the calm surface of a lake reflecting images of me and Tomáš.
That, however, had disappeared underground.
Tomáš tried to break through the blockade of eternity and bring us back to the present. "Listen, Shrimp, where will you go when you finish secondary school?
I was glad he had addressed me as he used to in the past—Shrimp.

---

3   A Slovak saying about the first snow arriving on St. Martin's Day (11th November)

I shrugged my shoulders. "I haven't thought about it yet."

"He's still got plenty of time," Uncle backed me up. Apparently, he didn't think we should be wasting precious time with idle talk. But I understood what Tomáš was trying to do. I read it in his eyes. He didn't want our conversation to come to an end. The time allotted for the visit was about up. Mum sensed that too. She looked as if she would faint. She turned pale and began to sweat. The woman officer had no doubt been watching her carefully, because before we noticed this, the guard stepped up to her and offered her a glass of water. And at the same time she quietly announced, "The visit is over."

Tomáš got up, but he reeled and sat down again. He tried to light a cigarette, but his hands were shaking and he couldn't open the matchbox. He looked at us ashamedly. The pupils of his eyes were incredibly wide; I had the feeling they were filling the whole room. I saw how he was begging Mum with his eyes to help him, to save him. But through his lips came sounds more like groans than words.

"Mum. Little brother. Tell Dad... Send him my love. Uncle, please help them. Goodbye. Bury me at home." He was clearly close to collapsing. He was still sitting; he probably hadn't the strength to get up.

"Goodbye and don't be afraid," said Uncle.

"The visit is over," repeated the woman officer.

Tomáš didn't react. He looked wide-eyed from Mum to Uncle; at that moment he seemed to have forgotten me.

The woman officer signalled with her gaze to the guards standing opposite. "Help him," she quietly ordered them. Putting a hand under each arm, they lifted him and dragged him towards the door. There they allowed him to turn round for the last time. This time, however, his wandering gaze picked me out first. I took it as a reproach. Why didn't one of us help him? I stood up and pressed my whole body against the wide, heavy table, until I managed to push it away a few centimetres. I don't know what I wanted to achieve. Perhaps I was unconsciously pushing away the walls of the prison to somewhere beyond us, into the darkness, into non-existence, and I cried out at the same time:

"Leave him alone! He's innocent. Let him go! Escape, Tomáš! Run away!" Someone strong put their hand over my mouth. A second later they pulled Tomáš through the green door of hopelessness. I thought I saw in his posture a faint sign of resistance. Mum fainted. I remember that one of the armed guards threw a glass of water in her face; my Švošov uncle held her in his arms and wiped her pale, perspiring face with a large white handkerchief. Mum soon came to and we sat her on a chair and waited until she herself said she felt better and we could go. The armed guards left and only the Chief Officer remained with us. It must have been about an hour after midnight. I, too, slowly recovered from that hitherto unnamed frame of mind. I no longer felt anything. No tiredness, no anxiety, sadness, anger, hopelessness, nothing. Only years later can I name that state. The child in me died. But it was only a clinical death. Even now I am doomed to die several times a day when I think of these events and of Tomáš. I saw him once more, now lifeless, in the morgue on that early, cold and damp morning during which they executed three condemned men. We spent the night waiting at the station, but at six we were already in the morgue. We had to hand the suit over to the official and arrange for the funeral at the parochial office. The death knell tolled long and mournfully at the nearby church. We three went into the church to pray. Did I pray, too? I don't know. An hour later we went back to the morgue. Mum took me by the hand and led me to an open coffin. I saw the sharp profile of a shaven head, the hands emerging from the black suit with silver stripes, laid motionless on the chest. It was the suit Tomáš had worn for his school graduation. Only when we stepped nearer did we realise that someone else was wearing it, an older man, a stranger. The mad hope that Tomáš and we too had been the victims of a cruel joke first made me burst out laughing and then crying.

"Our Tomáš is alive. Tomáš is alive!" I cried half-aloud, dancing and running between the coffins like a madman. Then my gaze fell on a naked body in a coffin by the wall, his white chest slit open then carelessly sewn up. The shaven head likewise. Tomáš! Good God! Tomáš!

We buried him the same morning. They didn't allow us to take him home. I don't remember the funeral or the mass for the dead. I do know, however, that sleet was falling. None of the people we met had any idea we were weeping.

That's all I, Ján, have to tell you. My testimony is confirmed by the written sentence and the record of execution, as well as the notes in my diary. Since then, however, I haven't continued writing it. I have come to realise that time is a more eloquent witness than a human being. The latter often repeats himself in his statements and is mistaken in his deductions, becoming a fly caught by a spider, demanding freedom more than life. Here I have an adult in mind. That is because a child is life's darling. He imagines life to be a meadow, forest or river, a hawk and deer, in exceptional cases also outer space. But imagine a boy for whom these attractive and exciting images are replaced by the picture of a grey building with barred windows, surrounded by a fence with barbed wire or a stone bulwark and watch towers, in which he can see men in uniforms with rifles in their hands. Freedom is the Achilles' heel of mankind. As only someone who is not free, in other words a slave, can lay down his life for freedom, there are few people who want to play this, at first glance undignified, role in life. And so the paradox arises: seemingly free judges condemn to death ostensibly unfree citizens, but in both cases this is only playing at freedom, just as life is only pretending to be life. After all, which person knows the real reason for their existence?

DEEP GREEN

A TALE OF GLOOM

THEY CAME. I guessed who they were at first sight. For a moment my mind was occupied with the question of why there are always two of them. Even in my dreams they come in twos. I still can't find an answer to why that is.

I was sitting under a flowering apple tree on a simple bench of roughly planed beech planks. There were hordes of bees buzzing up among the branches. Two suns glistened in the windows of my house facing westwards. Children were playing hide-and-seek in the street. From beyond the rectangles of the gardens came the whistle of a train. The breath of the evening was blowing through the wooden fence. A cool, lonely and above all untimely evening. However, I was the only one to see it that way. The suns in the windows of my house were laughing at me. Even the buzzing of the bees sounded mocking. Anxiety gripped my heart. A hot ray of light flashed through the darkness of my mind. Little bells of childhood fear tinkled somewhere in my ear. My distracted gaze fell on the gloomy green of the beet fields. Lit up by the sun, they glistened like the outstretched wings of a thousand silver butterflies. Yet in their stillness there was something eerie and magical at the same time. The tough beet leaves clung close to the ground, as if wanting to cover it completely to protect it from invisible, progressive decay. At the same time my nostrils caught the scent of freshly cut beet and molasses. Something sweet melted on my tongue and soon I recalled the taste of treacle toffee, the unrefined sugar, yellowish-black as a wasp that my father used to bring home from work during the sugar-beet harvest. My mother would store lumps of it in a jam jar. In the winter, when flu was rife and I had a cold, she would use it to sweeten my linden tea.

Here in my own backyard, behind the bulwark of my own self, from early spring to late autumn I can feast my eyes on green vegetation of all possible shades. Every day I test the devotion of the grass, when I trample over it in my boots, and urged on by a strange, even perverse humility, it lovingly hugs my ankles. In this it is like a woman who never tires of being kicked by her lover. And when I lie down beside it, its long supple tufts stroke my face and its bright green shines into my darkness.

My former treacle toffee autumn still floats in the pure, fragrant air like a feather from a shot bird. For the rest of my life it will descend to the ground and I shall prepare to meet it as if meeting a woman I love. That autumn everything is very familiar, like the flippant jibes of the children reaching me from the street. "Tonka's bonkers." "Jojo's a dodo," the girl chants back at the boy. Laughter and giggles are to be heard. It was something else, something more scornful they used to call after me: "Celo[4] swiped a fly with a cello".

I didn't, however, dare shout back at the jeerers and I couldn't quickly think up a witty and apt rhyme to retaliate with. I was a shy and lonely boy, the only son of a seasonal worker and a housemaid. My loneliness was increased by one more circumstance: I attended a grammar school, while all my peers went to the secondary school in the next village. I would trundle into town by train every day from Monday to Saturday. Thus I was living two lives—one as a village boy, one as a town boy, or to be more exact, as a student. It took me half an hour to get to the station. The narrow road chewed its way through the fields like a caterpillar through a cabbage leaf. Every day I had to run to catch the train. I

---

4   Pronounced "Tsello"

invariably spied it only at the last moment. It hid behind the houses and to me its invisible movement seemed unpredictable and malicious. One time the journey to school almost cost me my life.

After the war old German carriages were added to the trains; they had maybe eight or even ten doors and one step running the whole length of the carriage. I jumped onto one such carriage at the last minute when it was already moving. I pressed down the handle, but the door didn't open. It was stuck or locked; I rattled the handle in vain; it remained shut. Meanwhile the train picked up speed. Fortunately the trains didn't travel as fast then as they do nowadays, but even so, for an eleven-year-old boy it was an unenviable situation. I was standing on the step, clinging to the rattling carriage; what's more, it was January, so after a couple of minutes my hands were turning numb. I had no gloves; I couldn't warm them in my pockets, as I had to grip the vertical bar with one hand and hold on to my bag with the other. The carriage shuddered as it crossed the points and shook like a hay cart, and although my fingers were icy cold, I didn't let go of the metal rail; I clung tight, even when I felt my hand freezing to it. I was hanging on to the train on the side opposite to where people got off, so the guard didn't notice me. I slipped away from the station through a hole in the fence and joined the other passengers in the nearby park. The journey back was much easier. I usually sat in the last carriage and on warm days I preferred to stand on the open platform at the end.

The eight school autumns were almost identical. In my case, however, invisible time took on a concrete form. It assumed the appearance of a lively little person of uncertain age. Her name was Mrs Murinová and she was a flower seller. For the whole eight years I would meet her at the station or see her on the train holding a basket of perennial plants or a bucket with a bright mixture of flowers.

"You had to run to catch it again, Celo," she reproached me mildly, when she had seen me darting under the lowered barrier and leaping on to the train at the last moment. On the way back she would ask with gentle curiosity how I'd gone on at school. Sometimes, however, she refrained from asking when she saw from my expression that things hadn't gone too well for me that day.

That train crosses the landscape of my memory to this very day. And smoke still comes out of the red sugar-factory chimney year after year. During the sugar harvest, white clouds of steam rise from the evaporators. My memory has also retained a picture of my father moving in the area between the evaporators and the cauldrons. On Sundays when he happened to have the long—twelve-hour—shift, I used to bring him his Sunday lunch. I really looked forward to those Sundays because of the black treacle toffee. Father used to sit on the steel steps with his dish on his knees while I, with a sweet lump slowly dissolving in my mouth, peered through the little glass window behind which the mysterious transformation of beet into sugar was taking place. Thanks to my memory, the dust of those roads and pathways leaves a sweet taste in my mouth.

There are, however, other roads and paths. Their dust has a different taste. Every little stone kicked from under your feet has a different shape, colour, hardness and value. A stone falling from a height sends up a whirl of dust when it hits the ground, or it transforms a dirty puddle into a sparkling geyser. Everything, every single thing, even our souls, is left to the tender mercies of the moment, to the brightness of life or the blackness of death. We submerge ourselves in two seas, one of which means rebirth and the other extinction. The deep only seems to reach up to our ankles. Instead of seagulls the spirit of God soars over us. But are all paths the paths of God? Even this one that has brought these two to me?

The younger of the pair addressed me.

"Mr Bizub?"

"Yes."

The other told me why they had come.

There are truths you accept only later, when you have been able for some time to consider them blatant lies or fabrication. This was such a case. I was dumbstruck. I just stuttered, "But that can't be... it's not... true."

"Unfortunately, it is true," the first confirmed the words of the other. "You'll have to come with us, Mr Bizub," he added, as if by the way. Not a muscle in his face moved. His rather-too-long fair hair also lay motionless on the collar of his freshly-washed denim jacket.

I must go... Must I? When? Right now? Shouldn't I resist? What actually do they want from me? How dare they? My house is my castle. Who let them in? Why is the gate open? I had an urge to get up and go and shut it. I think I even made a move in that direction, but fortunately I thought better of it in time. Why are you scared?—I yelled at myself in my mind. I realised these two were watching me. No doubt the flush or paleness of my face did not escape their attention. I felt as if the skin on it was shrinking. I rubbed my forehead and cheeks. For some reason I was ashamed. Then I realised why. I was ashamed of my helplessness. "You will have to come with us." For me that sentence had the effect of a spell or a hypnotic. From it I could deduce the formula of my future, or my horoscope; from it I could begin to write out a new era in my life.

Milka leaned out of the kitchen window. I could see from her face that she was about to tell me something, but when she caught sight of those two, she stopped herself, just nodded a greeting and disappeared behind the net curtain. The men's attention was alerted.

"Your wife?" asked the first.

"We can go in if you like," I muttered instead of answering the question put in an official tone.

They both glanced at the bench they had made me get up from a few seconds earlier.

"It'll be better here," the second man said promptly. He bent towards the bench and ran his fingers over the brown-painted, cracked and somewhat gnarled planks. "At least we can talk uninterrupted here for a bit."

It didn't even occur to me to ask what they wanted to talk to me about. Instead, I assumed the role of host. "Please sit down." I sat down first. Out of the corner of my eye I saw the window curtain twitch. I could imagine Milka staring at us and wondering who these visitors were and what they wanted of me. Suddenly I longed for her to draw the curtain right back and lean out of the window, so that I could see and hear her. I had the feeling that my resistance and courage were seeping through some crack in me and the empty space they left was filling up with fear. I had been needing Milka more and more often lately and for a different reason each time. I still liked looking at her, stroking her with my gaze, even though it was a long time since she had been young and pretty. And I was amazed to think what a miraculous organ our eyes are with their ability to see the same thing in a different way each time, as if people have yet another pair of eyes, more clear-sighted and observant.

I'm probably still in love with my wife, but I don't know this for certain; that is, I'm not sure if I loved her at some time in the past and whether she loved me then. I was waiting for the train, sitting on a bench on platform two (the trains going eastwards still leave from there), I was brooding over myself, my life; I didn't know what to do with it, where to turn. It was easier for the rails than for me; they led somewhere, they seemed to converge at some point, the sun cast an eye on them, the railway signals flashed blue and red over them, the swallows were completely indifferent to them. They behaved the same way to me. Two days earlier I had come back from prison. For eight years I had been muttering behind barbed wire. An amnesty had set me free. I was eighteen when they locked me up, now I was a twenty-six year old man with the first grey hairs glistening in my thinning dark chestnut forelock. Two hours earlier I had presented myself to the police. They had behaved quite normally towards me. Neither they nor I felt much like talking. I was not the first or the last jailbird they had come into contact with recently.

"Have you got a job?"

"No."

"What do you want to do?"

"I don't know."

I had walked all over town, hoping to meet someone who would help me find a job, hoping I'd see a notice or advertisement of some kind promising suitable employment. No one wanted me. So I ended up at the station. I went into the transport office and offered the railway company my services. When I told some important railway official where I'd come from two days earlier, he didn't even bother to explain to me why they couldn't take me on, not even to unload wagons.

Then I sat down on the platform bench, listened to the rumblings of my own stomach and stared at the rails converging in the distance. I was rescued from these gloomy thoughts by a girl. She sat down next to me on the bench and asked me outright, "Going home from work, Celo?"

I looked at her in alarm. For eight years I hadn't seen any girl close up, to say nothing of one speaking to me. She was a twenty-year-old apparition with light-brown hair, striking lips (a little cracked), high cheek bones, long fingers and deformed knuckles. She gazed at me with coffee-coloured eyes that were overlarge for her face, but there was so much warmth and light in them that I felt the wax of loneliness and despair within me begin to melt. She smiled at me as a younger sister might when she wants to wheedle a few coins out of her older brother to buy ice cream.

"Yes. No!" I immediately corrected myself. I was bowled over by her. She knew me by name. Who, apart from my parents, still remembered that name? I could hardly manage to stutter, "You know me?"

She laughed in a pleasant, relaxed manner. "Of course I know you. Don't you remember me?"

I shrugged my shoulders. I didn't recognise her. I probably should have known her. How embarrassing! "You... you're...?" I looked a right idiot.

"Milka Opatovská, of course. We live next door."

She had been twelve when they locked me up and now she was a girl of marriageable age, a twenty year old woman. And I was now—according to my mother—a man ready for marriage. But was that really the case? It's true I was twenty-six, but I had never kissed a girl. Or, I had in fact—a classmate, Irča Španková, the daughter of a textile retailer. It had been her name day or birthday; she had offered the whole class chocolates and had even let the boys kiss her. I remember that kiss to this day: it tasted like cucumber. I remember her lips too: they were as yielding as mushy soil.

A few days later we saw her father standing in his own shop window with bales of cloth at his feet. Dangling on his chest was a cardboard notice: AND I STOLE ALL THIS FROM THE WORKING CLASS. It was a terrible sight. I don't know why his thin figure with his bald head sunk on his chest did not move anyone, and rather than sympathy, aroused only ridicule. Curious passers-by, dozens of whom stopped in front of the shop window that day, vied with each other in thinking up witty comments at the expense of the poor man in the window. Irča didn't come to school. Two days later, at a hastily summoned meeting in the school gym, we expelled her from the youth organisation. I didn't, however, raise my hand when they voted. Expulsion from the grammar school followed. None of us stood up for her. Only Lýdia Gavurová timidly remarked that it was not fair for children to suffer for their parents.

Form leader Bohuš Králik advised her to kindly mind her own business. "Your father has also got something to answer for," he reminded her.

"What? What something?"

"He's a *kulak*!" Bohuš shouted triumphantly. "A class enemy."

At that time the newspapers were writing almost every day about *kulaks*, about trials of class enemies, conspiratorial centres and bourgeois nationalists.

Lýdia sat down at her desk and burst into tears. Not one of the girls dared comfort her. Tall, slim and fair-haired Irča disappeared from my life. She became a hair fallen from the incredibly thick shiny mane of humankind. In her place, ten years later, another girl, returning from work in the clothing factory, sat down beside me on platform two. Since then she has been zooming along in my life like the needle of a sewing machine. She has managed to mend a few tears in my soul. Her industriousness and persistence still fascinate me to this day. But sometimes the touching devotion with which she hangs on me like a late apple on a tree gets on my nerves. Then I treat her roughly, badly. I have a strong urge to shake her off but fortunately, have not succeeded. At such times she asks me more with her eyes than with her mouth why I am hurting her.

"I don't know what got into me," I make insincere excuses. In fact I did know. We were two Bizubs. I hardly know the other one; I don't know what he is capable of. He keeps stalking me from inside. I'm scared of him and he's scared of me.

My answer does not satisfy Milka. "Tell me what you've got against me!"

I shake my head. I'm not prepared to reply out loud. After such times I usually feel dead exhausted. I've had moments when I would have departed this life without regret.

Milka doesn't leave it at that. "What's troubling you? You can tell me."

I have always been ashamed to entrust another with my troubles. When I got back from prison my mother asked me what it was like. I said it was bearable. Really. Sometimes you felt rotten, but occasionally a strange euphoria kept you afloat, a mixture of inert gases that protected you from destruction. It's like that in life: at one time you are plodding along in heavy boots and can barely drag your feet, at other times you are walking on tiptoe and everything you see is like in a dream. There were some who managed to switch off their thoughts and allow snow to fly around in their minds instead. By morning the snow had lined their souls and they died in peace.

Coming home after such a long absence is something not many people experience. It is a celebration of birth as well as a funeral. For a while you feel as if you had left home only a few days ago, but a day or two later you realise that your whole life has turned on its axis as it does for a sick man on his death bed. On the surface nothing had changed. Our old house was standing in its place between other houses that all looked alike. I knocked on the door. No one invited me to enter. Only in my memory could I hear my mother's clear call: "The door's open. Come in, please." My folks weren't expecting me. They didn't believe they'd let me go; they didn't dare hope I would return home. It was two o'clock in the afternoon. I found the key to the house in the old place: under the electricity meter, among the burned-out fuses and an old padlock from the garden gate. I had lost the key to it years ago, so I had had to saw through it with a metal file. Ever since then it had been useless, but I remembered Dad's "it may come in handy one day" and I immediately understood why it had remained in the same old place. I unlocked the door, went into the kitchen and put my bundle down on the table with the couple of things I had recently bought in the camp. Above all, I'd had to buy something to wear, because in those eight years I had grown out of what I was wearing when they locked me up. Apart from socks, shirts and one tie I had also brought three books. Everything about me was new. Not only was I four centimetres taller, more robust and certainly stronger, I was also someone quite different, changed inside.

I went out into the vegetable garden. Nettles waist high along the fence—just like years ago. Their bitter scent filled me with sadness. Bees circled over my head and I kept having to drive them away. The pear and apple trees were covered with pink and white blossoms. I realised that the bees were attracted by the smell of my clothes. They smelt of newness, mothballs and formaldehyde. The amnesty was a stroke of good fortune for the clothes merchants. Thousands of prisoners threw off their prison uniforms and could dress like human beings. It was a wonderful feeling, but at the same time painful: the feeling of a person coming round from an anaesthetic. And along with the joyful realisation that he is still alive, he discovers that in order to save his life half his lungs have been removed. To pass the time I walked among the rows of parsley, carrots, onions and kohlrabi. I touched the shaggy green fronds and thought about my mother. She had probably popped out to the shop. I knew my father went to work. In spring and summer he worked in the brick factory and in autumn in the sugar factory. In my time the working hours at the brickworks were from seven to three. If it was still the same my father would be arriving in about an hour. My mother, however, should appear any time now.

I was not mistaken. She came looking for me in the vegetable garden. She knew where to find me. She guessed that with its feeling of freedom the open space behind the barns would be the first place to take me in its arms. What did it matter that this space was not an endless expanse, but just a little piece of flat land? Freedom is everyone's territory, but it doesn't belong to anyone. Yet my feeling of freedom was very much like anxiety. The open space beyond the fence depressed me. I stood facing freedom, with my back to my mother. She had to come right up to me and timidly poke my back with one finger to make me turn round. She couldn't speak. To the last moment she didn't believe it was me. Tears ran down her face, wetting my cheek and the collar of my brand new beige shirt. She hugged me so tightly we staggered. She groaned from pain and happiness. It was my second arrival in the world. For several seconds the valley of tears was transformed into a garden of paradise. After those few seconds my mother tore herself away and spoke at last. "You came back. The Lord God heard my prayers. Now I can die."

At that time I did not understand why she poured ink into that white moment. Could she have seen testimony to her life in a dream or written on the pages of her lonely soul? She died two years later, also in May, and my father survived her by less than a year.

Slowly, not speaking, we returned to the yard. A striped ginger cat came to rub herself against my legs. She did the same to my mother, only with the difference that she turned her head towards her and blinking and quietly miaowing she begged for food. Mother went into the kitchen and brought her a mug of milk. She poured it into a battered tin bowl and went out into the street to see if my father was returning from work.

Dad came a few minutes later. Someone had run over to the brickworks to bring him the news of my arrival. Someone I did not know, but who knew me. He hurried inside. But first he scooped up a mug of water from the bucket, drank and only then did he hold out his hand.

"Welcome."

That was all. He sat down at the table and lit a cigarette. It pierced my heart. I couldn't see any emotion in his face. He only showed he was hungry and thirsty. The austere expression on my father's face confused me for a long time; I fought hard not to take it the wrong way. Only later did I understand that in my presence he was ashamed of his helplessness. He hadn't been able to help his child. And no matter whether it is a child drowning in a river or endangered by the flames of a burning house, this feeling of helplessness hurts fathers more than mothers.

Mum watched this scene with a smile. She knew my father better than me. She leaned up against the sideboard and couldn't tear her eyes away from me. Suddenly she snapped out of her reverie.

"Goodness me! You haven't eaten yet."

I was so hungry I could have eaten a horse.

The two sit beside me, one on each side. My charge is written in their expressions. They know as well as I do that no one is blameless, no one is completely innocent. Under certain circumstances my indictment could be read as a speech for the defence, or an appeal against the sentence. Everything that until now made for peace, a feeling of security and the strange reconciliation of a human being with himself, when a person is invisibly becoming restored and reaching his depths, is examining thoughts about himself, which—unfortunately—are often a source of shame and false pride, now turned against me.

The thirty-year-old who was sitting on my right, the one with ever-quivering nostrils, a slim detective, asked me where I had first met Hoffart.

"In the camp. In fifty-five. He escaped in February fifty-six and we haven't seen each other since."

"You saw each other last Saturday," the other man sitting on my left reminded me. Broad-shouldered, with a wide, sincere face and muscular chest—a bodybuilder most likely. Protector of innocent girls and old men.

"He phoned you," the detective added. He lifted his head, poking his nose in the air. "You haven't got a telephone!" he said, visibly disappointed with his discovery. They looked at each other reproachfully. They'd messed something up. Of course! They hadn't checked whether I had a telephone or not. They'd only found out that we'd spoken together over the phone. It was the detective who went on with the interrogation. He probably wanted to make up for what he'd let slip.

"Did he call you at work?"

"I'm retired," I replied. And thought with malicious glee: They're slackers. They didn't even check whether or not I had a phone.

"So where the devil did he sniff you out then?"

"He rang the post office. They let me know when he would call."

"Thursday at 8 pm?"

"Why ask if you already know?"

"For the record."

I didn't tell them that I hadn't had to go as far as the post office to take the call. Three houses down from us lives Milka's classmate, Anka Guzmová; she works at the post office and she has a telephone. She arranged for the call to be put through to her. Our children occasionally take advantage of the possibility of calling us at her house. Our son is working in Bratislava, in a chemical factory and our daughter is in Košice, married to a professional soldier. Neither Jojo nor Miriam leave messages for calls at the post office. To tell the truth, this way of phoning had made me uneasy. A suspicion crossed my mind that I didn't dare share with Milka. What if it was a hospital calling? But they send telegrams; I comforted myself with the most acceptable answer. So who could be calling me? I racked my brains over it all afternoon. The postwoman had thrust the notice of the call into my hand outside the shop. It could have been about a quarter past one. Like today, it had been a beautiful day. But on that occasion the notice had torn the day to shreds. I was on tenterhooks until evening came. That notice magnetized Milka, too. She kept looking at the clock on the wall. At half past five she asked me whether I'd have some tea.

It was a good idea. She's always sure to guess when to take action. Then she steps into the empty space in my mind and offers my weary blood refreshment.

It was ten minutes to eight when I got out of my armchair. I didn't want Milka to go with me. I caught a glimpse of the beet fields shining through the open window. They looked like a lake. In them the gloom would soon become an abyss.

"I'm sorry to bother you," I apologised to Anka Guzmová. My gaze immediately fell on the telephone. To me it looked like a hand grenade with the safety pin pulled out.

"Why should you be sorry?" She lifted the receiver and dialled the number.

"Maja, give me that call from Bratislava." Anka had a pleasant voice. Quite a pretty little woman, just a bit too slim for my liking. All sinew. By contrast, her husband was as round as a beer barrel. She handed me the receiver. "You've got Bratislava," she said and discreetly disappeared from the kitchen.

A man's distant voice somewhere at the other end of the world was melancholically calling: "Hello. Hello. Hello." He infected me and I paid him back in the same coin.

"Hello."

The voice at the other end of the continent brightened up. "Hello!" it sang sweetly.

"Hello," I echoed dully.

"Who's there?" The foreign accent in that voice could be detected like garlic in goulash.

"Bizub," I said. "Who's calling?"

"Hoffart. Peter."

The name meant nothing to me. And yet I had a feeling it was like a burnt stain on the bottom of the pot of my memory. Hoffart? My brain began to turn slowly on its axis. It examined clues, sniffed at the decades, browsed through yellowing files. Hoffart?

"What do you want, please, Mr Hoffart?"

"Celo? Celo Bizub?"

"Celo." I recalled a game from childhood... Warm, warm, cold, cold. I felt hot. Beads of sweat poured down my forehead. A little stream flowed down my back. At the other end of the wire (I don't know why I imagine a wire stretched out between me and the caller) hoarse laughter could be heard. The trail in my memory was becoming clearer and clearer. I was confused by the fact that this laughter sounded bawdy, unfamiliar, really disgusting. Then a face flashed in the mirror of my memory.

"Kamagore!" I cried out aghast.

"I've found you at last." Hoffart stopped laughing. The relief in his voice was the answer to all my as yet unspoken questions. "I was beginning to think you were no longer alive. I'm really glad I've found you, kamagore."

"In the camp everyone called him Kamagore," I said. "Kamagore?" The fellow on my right slowly shook his head, mystified. "That's nonsense. Do you know what that word means?"

Should I explain to him that I had never tried to discover the meaning of that word? For me it had a universal meaning. It was a form of address, a greeting, a curse, an oath, a secret instruction. It didn't mean anything, and yet it meant everything. And on each occasion I understood it differently. It belonged to my prison life, like the mess tin, blanket and the number I'd been assigned, A025229. For as long as I live I shall remember it. To the end of my life I shall not forget the gate through which I entered the camp, even though they were almost all the same. Beyond it you find yourself in a completely new world, in another universe. You feel eyes crawling over you like ants, examining the properties of the juices you secrete. They are not tender gazes that soothe. Those stares tear the skin off you; they want to chafe until you bleed, to determine your blood group. In them you can see curiosity, indifference and also disappointment that you have not met their expectations and presuppositions. Meanwhile you realise that no one has been expecting you and no one is glad you have come.

I felt really lonely, a foreigner in a strange land. I felt uncomfortable, but with the passing minutes I became increasingly convinced that the worst was over. After months of solitary confinement the camp began to seem like a reward. I studied my wrists; a red stripe could still be seen, left by the handcuffs. In the bus we had sat chained together, man to man in uneven pairs, the prison guards with machine guns sitting facing us, their eyes fixed on us throughout the journey lasting several hours. When we arrived at the camp they unlocked our fetters and let us into the space in which each of us would find his own little patch.

One of the heads of the camp, a short, healthy-looking forty-year old, holding a paper in his right hand, called out our names in a voice that resounded like a sheet of galvanized metal.

"Bizub! Which of you is Bizub?" I raised my hand. "I'm Bizub."

"Number A025229. Remember that number, Bizub." "I'll remember. A025229." It immediately engraved itself on my memory. It was quite an easy number to remember.

"Hut B, room number ten, Bizub. That's the hut on the right, at the end of the row. Go to your accommodation."

Trembling, I did as I was told. I had to parade past the assembled unit. I elbowed my way through the crowds of indifferent figures lining the way to the hut with its encoded air of loneliness. I entered room number ten just at the moment when one of a pair of chess players sitting at the table quietly declared: "Checkmate."

"Good afternoon," I said timidly.

Six pairs of eyes drive through me like a lorry loaded with wet sand. I feel as if I've been put in a pillory. The six men are on their guard. They are watching my every movement and may even be subconsciously analysing my scent. My instinct of self-preservation is telling me to defend myself.

"I'm Bizub," I introduced myself. Who knows why in doing so I raised my voice. I immediately considered this to be my first false step. I had wanted to shield myself with that most ineffective and unreliable weapon—my own name.

The long silence reminded me of the family of the deaf mute tailor in our village. The film that someone had stopped moved on at last. A tall man with smoothly-combed light brown hair stepped towards me. He held out his hand.

"Markovič." Instinct told me that I was standing in front of a teacher. "A student?" My new acquaintance guessed my identity at first go.

I nodded shamefacedly and also gladly. I had always felt shy in the presence of teachers. Gladly, because I felt that I was gradually surfacing from my depths. I felt safer. Apart from that, the cage I now found myself in was spacious. All this time I had not let go of my rucksack. Someone gently took it from me and put it on the top berth of the metal bunk bed I was standing next to.

A chess player. About thirty. He had a freckled face and reddish eyebrows and hair. "You're young, you can sleep up there."

I shook hands with the rest of them. A small fairhaired man of indeterminate age was kneeling in the space between the beds. He was clearly praying. I hesitated. I didn't know whether I could disturb him just then. However, he got to his feet and smiled at me. He looked at me with eyes as blue as the sky and in a voice that sparkled like water he asked me in Czech what my Christian name was.

"Celestín. Celo," I whispered gratefully. It had been a long time since anyone had asked me my first name.

"Nice name," he said. "Who were you named after? Your father?"

"My father's Jozef."

"I'm Josef too. Josef Heřman. And I'm a Catholic priest." Only then did he offer me his hand. It was small, soft and its clasp was like a print in the snow of my soul. He kept gazing at me with those incredibly blue eyes, the kind only children have. He could easily have used that gaze instead of his hands. "How much did the People's Court give you, lad?"

"Eighteen," I said uneasily.

"Eighteen months or years?"

"Years," I confessed.

Once more six pairs of eyes glanced at me. They brushed against me like butterfly wings. No one asked why I had been thrown into jail. Later I also learned to read that strange, invisible writing, the language of eyes and gestures. Thanks to that I was able to distinguish a farmer from a teacher, pick out a thief and a homosexual, and identify a murderer. At that time I was only just entering the world of adult men, moving around in it with the uncertainty of a calf that has only been an hour or two in this world. Surrounded by hundreds of noble-minded, courageous men, the murderers and thugs must have suffered terribly; they underwent a real re-education process and many of them were inwardly changed. I was freed from my discomfiture by another newcomer, a small, lively man of about sixty with a face like a walnut. He immediately and unashamedly confessed his past.

"I'm Franta Brabec, a thief, but I don't steal in the jug."

Some responded to his words with a smile, others looked disconcerted. Then they invited me to join them at the table, offering me tea and biscuits.

"Help yourself. Don't be shy."

"Take more sugar. Sugar will put you back on your feet."

I drank some tea and thought of treacle toffee and my father. I crunched cocoa biscuits and thought of my mother and the hot cocoa we had in school a couple of months after the war. It had all gone smoothly. I felt like a chess player who has won an important game without knowing how to move the pieces. I was a beginner. Beginners don't mind losing. I had found myself in an artificial world. In a warm lair, from which I was driven out by the evening roll call and supper, the blaring of loudspeakers calling on those on duty in the huts to announce preparations for supper and lights out.

With an endless feeling of relief I stretched out on my bunk. I fell asleep like a newborn baby. An hour before midnight I was woken up by a pitiless stomping of heavy boots and the clatter of mess tins. The afternoon shift had returned. Men with mess tins were hurrying to collect their supper; they too wanted to get the day over as soon as possible and were longing to rest after jumping off the merry-go-round of endless days and nights of toil and roll calls. The light switch clicked and a blinding lamp flooded the room with restrained light, in which I saw for the first time in my life the pitiful figure and face of a prematurely aged man of about twenty-five with deeply sunken eyes, a scar that cut his chin and lower lip into two elongated, ugly segments.

"New?" he asked me in gruff voice. I couldn't see the slightest hint of sympathy in his greenish brown eyes. And when he opened his mouth, my gaze fell into the black opening he'd been left with in lieu of teeth. He was the neighbour opposite me. He also slept on the top bunk.

"Bizub," I muttered, offering my hand.

He completely ignored my gesture. He took his mess tin and went for supper. I don't know when he came back. Once again I managed to fall asleep. I was woken by the rattle of the bed, a thud, hubbub and cursing. Someone turned on the light. Half the occupants had been woken up by the noise, the other half pretended to be asleep. My neighbour was picking himself up off the oiled floor, feeling his banged elbow and right arm.

"Think I must've slipped off my bed," he observed laconically. And when he caught sight of me watching him sympathetically, he laughed. "Be careful you don't do the same, *kamagore*."

Kamagore! That's some Italian, I thought disappointedly. He's probably calling me a *magor*—a screwball.

The plain clothes officer sitting on my right got up, stretched himself and then turned on the tap. The water, falling from the height of a metre onto the concrete drain, splashed merrily. A hose lay in the grass like a sleeping black snake. The plain-clothes policeman quickly washed his hands and drank from his palms.

"You should have said you were thirsty," I said peevishly.

"We stopped for lunch. It was a bit too salty."

"Really? I didn't notice," the body builder said in surprise.

Until then he had listened intently to what I was saying. Now there was a danger of interrupting the contact he had managed to establish with me. "But if you're bored, go and wait in the car." His colleague hadn't exactly chosen the best moment to quench his thirst, so he made this clear. But the other one had obviously lost interest in my story.

"Can't he tell us on the way back, Captain?"

"You needn't advise me what to do," the body builder put an official end to the dispute with his subordinate. His irritated colleague waved a hand resignedly, sat down on the edge of the bench with his back to us and, facing the road, he watched the children, while perhaps half listening to our conversation.

"Were you glad he'd remembered you?"

It wasn't easy to reply to this seemingly simple question. First I had to sort out in my head the mixture of feelings that were whirling me round like water turning a mill wheel. But the water that flooded over me was icy cold and not very clean. My immediate reaction had been to slam down the receiver and dash out of Anka Guzmanová's house without a word of explanation and roam through the fields till morning, crawl in among the beet leaves and from there gaze at the falling stars. However, I'd taken a grip on myself, curiosity finally helping me.

"How did you find me?"

"Easily." He laughed triumphantly. "I went to the post office, I gave them your address and they took care of the rest."

"After all these years you remembered the name of the village where I lived?"

"My memory's still good," he boasted jovially.

The satisfaction, confidence and pride I sensed in his voice hurt me and made me feel ashamed. I realised he was decades ahead of me, of my life. He had clearly long been free of pangs of conscience and painful memories, while I would probably reach that state of mind only in the hour of my death. I almost began to envy him. But then I stuck out my claws after all. "I'm surprised you felt like bothering," I remarked rudely.

"We're buddies, aren't we?"

"Depends how you look at it."

"What's the matter? What's up, kamagore?" He was probably beginning to guess. "You can't be angry with me, can you?"

Idiot! Stupid jerk! Jackass! I mentally swore at him. He hadn't understood a thing! The old disappointment gave me new pain. I had no idea all that could come back again after so many years. And not only the disappointment, but also the knowledge that he had been my closest friend, that I had been fond of him, that even now I had not forgotten him. Not only had he taught me to smoke and to roll cigarettes but he had managed to make a different man of me, to convert me to his faith, teaching me to trust my own strength, giving my life a different meaning. No one else had managed to do that, neither the teacher nor the priest, to say nothing of the prison screws.

Kamagore! Everyone called him that. We came from very different backgrounds, but we were of a similar age. He was my older brother, my protector, while the other guys were my fathers and they never became my buddies. His mother had a chemist's or perfumery in Bratislava; he rarely mentioned his father, a German who had been conscripted and taken captive and not been heard of since. He really hated the man his mother got together with after the war. "You've no idea how his feet stank," he complained to me with a laugh. "That's why I fled over the border!" Once a guard named Človíček[5] dragged him out of bed. That was because Kamagore had lain down and fallen asleep an hour before lightsout. Človíček was running through the huts checking the rooms were tidy. He discovered the sleeper and ordered us to wake him up.

I shook Kamagore's foot.

"What's up? Why're you waking me?"

"You've got to get up."

Kamagore lifted himself onto his elbow.

"How do you come to be sleeping?" the screw yelled at him.

"I'm not sleeping, officer," muttered Kamagore. He sat up on the bed and swung his legs right under the officer's nose. The latter stepped backwards in horror.

"Boy, you haven't washed your feet! Go and wash them!"

Kamagore obediently slipped down from the bed, pulled on his boots, took a towel and went off to the washroom. Meanwhile Človíček went through his bed and metal locker. By some lucky chance he didn't notice a packet of cigarettes lying next to the mess tin. You see, the camp's canteen didn't stock that brand of cigarettes.

---

5 "little man" or "boy"

Kamagore came back from the washroom, halted two paces from Človíček, drew his right foot out of his boot and held it out.

"It doesn't smell now, officer. Take a sniff."

This was too much for Človíček. Kamagore's insolence cost him ten days' solitary confinement. In that regard I was dead lucky. So far I hadn't got into any scrapes. The kindly, fatherly affection of my older fellow prisoners helped me in this. From time to time the teacher would put his arm around my shoulders and stroke my cheek with his fingers. I was smooth-faced; I was shaved for the first time by the official barber before my court hearing. Kamagore didn't like it. "If he tries anything with you, tell me. I'll sock him one and he'll leave you alone. That's what works with queers."

I didn't understand anything. I was naïve and innocent. After some time I even began to feel my innocence to be a burden, an unwanted inheritance. I came to manhood in an environment where there were no women, and because I was working in the mines, I only managed to catch a brief and rare glimpse of the couple of older women working on the surface. However, memories of women flew around in the loneliness of our souls like night moths. While I could only select from the treasure box of my memory the taste of one girl's kiss, Kamagore, who had spent two years in Algeria, was marked body and soul by the pleasures of brothels and opium dens. While I would listen open-mouthed to the sparkling voice of Father Josef, Kamagore couldn't stand it and always went out of the room into the corridor and that way show him his contempt for God. Before Christmas the teacher only escaped ending up under a roof fall by a miracle. A few seconds earlier he had thought someone was calling him, so he switched off the drill and went into the main gallery to see whether the boy from transport wasn't calling him, because they were due to bring some props. That call, as it turned out, was the call of the teacher's guardian angel.

"God is always present in the life of each person," said Father Josef.

Kamagore objected irritably, "Rubbish! God doesn't care a shit about us."

The priest looked at him with a radiant gaze. We all saw it. Darkness had fallen early and we had been sitting in the gloom for some time. That gaze settled on Kamagore's scarred cheek as quietly as a bird. "One day you too will feel the touch of God's hand on your head, lad," he said calmly.

Kamagore let out a hoarse laugh, the same as the one I heard over the phone almost forty years later. He pointed to his crooked nose, his scar and knocked-out teeth. "No, thank you. It has already touched me. That was enough, Father."

It seemed at first that I had nothing in common with Kamagore. That's what the other occupants of the room thought too. They didn't like Kamagore. He was quick-tempered and rude, he spoke in a vulgar manner, he couldn't stand the quiet conversation of adults that flowed like a babbling brook, nor the animated stream of words that crystallised into surprising meanings. Even though I was only a student who hadn't yet finished grammar school, here and there I did manage to decode some of them. Kamagore, according to his own admission, had hardly managed to finish elementary school and was already chasing whores in Vydrica[6] when he was only fifteen.

He emigrated in '49. In France he let himself be recruited into the legions, but he quickly had enough of them; he spent some time in Austria, crossing the border a couple of times to visit his mother, and in the end they nailed him in '52, gave him twenty years, first sticking him in Leopoldov jail, then sending him to mine uranium. In the setting in which we found ourselves we were aliens. Even I didn't understand everything our elder brothers or fathers were talking about. I listened to them all and I was happy when I managed to understand some of what they were saying. Most of their stories were exciting and almost

---

6   Before and just after WWII Bratislava's red-light district

unbelievable. Milanovič had been sentenced to death in Yugoslavia by the Germans in '44. He had only managed to escape by the skin of his teeth, when partisans raided the prison and freed the inmates. After the war he became secretary at the Yugoslav embassy in Prague. There he was arrested in '52 and again sentenced to death. He appealed to the High Court and as both Stalin and Gottwald had died in the meantime, Milanovič got off with a life sentence. Father Josef spent the war in Buchenwald concentration camp, Sum was a Scout leader, Zábrana a Member of Parliament, Markovič a grammar school teacher, Vahovský a small farmer, the communist Evžen Deputy Minister of Finance. These men had already lived a good part of their lives; they understood politics, while we two had no past and did not dare speak aloud of the future.

The secret policeman wrote something down in his notebook. This time he didn't mark it with his finger, but closed it and shoved it into his pocket. He looked at his watch: "Three o' clock. High time we got a move on if we're going to manage it today." He looked me over speculatively. It was clear he wasn't happy about something.

"You should get changed, Mr Bizub."

I was wearing tracksuit trousers and a shirt. "I've told you all I know."

"You're the only person who can reliably confirm that the dead person found in Bratislava is Peter Hoffart and no one else."

Must I? I must. So we shall meet yet again, Kamagore.

I have had some strange good luck in my life. I have not been disappointed in love. And equally strange bad luck: the only friend I had in my life betrayed me. I'd got over my anger long ago, but the rest remained. I jumped after you into the water and you didn't hold out your hand to me when I began to drown. For you such things were just the usual twists and turns in your life. You laughed when I said so over the phone.

"You mustn't take it so tragically," he told me.

"It was a foul thing to do."

"Surely after so many years you're not going to hold something against me that I really couldn't help."

"I shall hold it against you until you too realise it was a foul thing to do," I insisted.

For a moment you were quiet. I was already beginning to think you really were pondering my words. But then I heard a girlish giggling in the receiver. And you whispering "Stop that. Can't you see I'm on the phone?" If I'd been standing next to you then, I would've killed you. At last you spoke up. "Okay. I admit it was a foul thing to do. But let's say no more about it, okay? I want to see you. Can you come to Bratislava? If you can, do come. I'm asking you to. Apart from you, I've got no one I can talk to."

The sincerity of your invitation touched me. In it I heard the call of a lonely person, the desperate cry of a child who has suddenly found himself in a busy street without his parents and siblings. "On Saturday?" I suggested uncertainly.

"Fine. You got a car?"

"Any idea where I'd get one?"

"I'll send a taxi for you."

"What are buses and trains for?"

"As you like. When will you be arriving?"

"Around noon."

"Fine. We'll have lunch together. I'm staying at the Devín Hotel. You know where it is?"

"Not exactly." It was twenty years since I'd been to Bratislava. "But I'll find it."

"At the reception desk tell them you've come to see me."

On purpose I said, "Yes, Kamagore."

"Mr Hoffart," he corrected me.

"Yes, Mister," I aped him. At the same time I remembered my three years of English at grammar school. My teachers and classmates too. Goodness, what a long time ago that was!

The mist in my mind had cleared. In it flashed Kamagore's slightly astigmatic eyes, with the black spot in the depths of the yellowish-green iris. They reminded me of the cut that makes a diamond special and more precious.

I went off to change. Only a week before, Milka had got me ready for a journey and now I would be asking her to do it again. There was an alabaster white limousine awaiting me outside the house. The plain-clothes officers were already sitting in it and talking to the driver. They were nothing like the pair three decades earlier. It was October then, a cold wind was blowing and sparrows were quarrelling over a bit of bread between the rails. I was on my way home from school and had just got off the train. The train was already past the signals, but the engine had left a cloud of black smoke over the station. Suddenly someone spoke to me. I tore my eyes away from the sparrows and my gaze met an obstacle: two tall, well-built men in long leather coats were standing before me. They looked like twins. I had never seen them before in my life. One of them gripped my arm above the elbow on the side where I was holding my bag. The other ran his hands over my body, frisking all my pockets. It didn't take him long. I was quite shabbily dressed in beige corduroys and a black twill jacket handed down from my uncle. I didn't resist or even protest against their actions. I was paralysed, taken unawares and as if unconscious. My reflexes, my blood, my whole demeanour betrayed me. I was only aware of the merciless, increasingly painful grip of the hand above my elbow. The men said something, I could see it by their lips, but I didn't hear a word of it. It all shot through me like a bullet from a revolver. It went straight through me; my brain hadn't yet registered it.

Then came the second shot. This one I now heard.

"Mr Bizub?"

The form of address confused me. Mr Bizub—no one had ever called me that before. I was too young for such a title. My first thought was that they had mistaken me for my father. They might have been looking for him and not found him at home. The sugar harvest was in full swing and that week my father had the afternoon shift. Mum was elsewhere, digging beet. When I get home now I'll find a note on the kitchen table: We're digging beet, I've taken the spade.

The other man at last stopped frisking me. He stood up in front of me and the gaze he rested on me was as heavy as stone. He said, "I arrest you in the name of the law, Bizub. I advise you not to resist and not to try to escape. It would be futile and what's more, we would be forced to use our weapons."

I understood absolutely nothing. I didn't even associate these men with the saloon car that was standing at the edge of the road a little higher up. The one gripping my arm let go at last. He asked me to hand over my bag and he looked inside it. All I had there was a pencil case, a couple of exercise books and two textbooks—physics and chemistry. I was still convinced that it was all a mistake, that they were looking for my father. But I didn't even try to think of a way to warn him of the danger. On this occasion Mrs Murínová had not been travelling with me; she had probably sold all her flowers before noon and gone home by the earlier train. And who knows whether she would have noticed anything; it all took place so quickly and inconspicuously, in the course of three or four minutes.

I stood like a pillar of salt; I glanced from right to left and left to right; I must have looked like an idiot to them, because in the end they grasped me by the arms, dragged me to the car and pushed me into the back seat. One of the men got in beside me. The car was already started, but instead of the hum of the running engine, I heard the crazy beating of my own heart; I felt the blood flowing from it, rushing into my arms and legs, bringing oxygen to my lungs and penetrating my brain. The saloon lurched as it moved off. We did a U-turn in the road and crossed the railway lines. I still didn't understand the significance of all this. We flew through the nearby town. It was getting dark. There were lights in the windows of the rooms in the *Pod skalou* Hotel. I glimpsed a light in one of the grammar school windows too. Once out of town the man sitting next to me stuck a cigarette in his mouth and clicked his lighter. I jerked my head away. The flame flared up near my face. I remembered how I had smoked with some boys in the school toilets and again with other boys on the open platform at the end of the last train carriage. That time I had walked part of the way with Mrs Murínová. I had no idea that hair could catch smells. Suddenly she stopped.

"You stink of cigarettes, Celo," she said out of the blue.

"The other boys were smoking," I said uncertainly.

"Only the other boys?"

"I just had a drag."

I was riding in a car for the first time. It may have been the feeling of dread, or maybe the cigarette smoke that made me want to vomit.

"Stop, please, I feel sick," I managed to mutter.

The one who was smoking pulled down the window and threw the half-finished cigarette out of the car, yelling in alarm: "Stop, or he'll puke all over me, the bloody swine."

He stood behind me while I vomited into the ditch. It didn't take long. I hadn't eaten anything since the morning. My lunch was waiting for me on the stove at home: cottage-cheese noodles. Huddled up in the back seat, I watched the black silhouettes of the trees flashing past me. I was tempted to stick out my hand and catch hold of their firm trunks. In the twilight the white reflector posts exploded like detonators. The blue facades of houses in the villages we were passing through looked darker and darker. The hills in the distance took on a purple hue. Clouds slid over the landscape, chasing each other. A drop of rain glistened on the windscreen. Then a couple drummed on the hood of the car and that was all there was of the rain. I desperately searched my mind for some comforting memory of rain. I couldn't find a single one. At that time in my life I could draw on lamentably few memories. Several years later I would be able to spread them like butter on my daily bread. The events I would experience would begin to seem boring and unimportant. Those raindrops on the windscreen soaked into me. At the same moment my anxiety came to the boil like water for tea. My survival instinct kicked in at last.

"Where are you taking me?"

"You'll find out."

"I haven't done anything."

"That's what they all say."

I began to jiggle the door handle and shout, "Let me go! Stop! I haven't done anything!" I know it was a childish, naïve attempt to change my situation.

The man sitting next to me put me in handcuffs. The more I jerked my hands, the deeper they cut into my wrists. At the same time I was yelling, "Let me go! Stop! Open the door!"

The man sitting in front turned round. "Shut your trap or I'll shut it for you!"

I was on the edge of tears, but I didn't start crying. I remembered my mother. Ondrej Poludvorný cut my head with a stone and my mother had hushed me with the words, "Don't cry, Celo. Big boys don't cry." I was ten years old then. Now I was eight years older. I had no right whatsoever to cry. Nevertheless, one day I would break down sobbing when my buddy left me to my fate.

Milka immediately asked me who those two were and what they wanted from me.

"They're from the police," I replied briefly. "It's about Kamagore. You needn't worry about me."

She turned pale, her eyes darting here and there as if caught up by a wind. I know that look very well. That wind is the wind of anxiety.

It had settled in her heart and she has carried it around with her ever since we set out on our journey together through life. She was taking sharp breaths and her chin began to tremble. These were clear signs of the onset of hysteria. Poor Milka! She had been wiping the spit off my body for many years and never found it repulsive. Even in my final hour she will sit beside my deathbed and wipe the last drops of anxiety from my forehead. She would be willing to stand before a firing squad if they were aiming the barrels of their rifles at me. "Bizub? Is that the man who served time with you?" It was the badge I wore on my chest instead of a yellow star. Maybe these two had come to see me for the same reason. I had been in prison; why couldn't I be Kamagore's murderer?

"Surely they can't have come to arrest you?" she asked quietly.

I laughed. "That's all I'd need. I must get changed."

She handed me a shirt. A striped one.

"No, not that one. Give me a plain one."

"What are you going to wear?"

"Black trousers and my tweed jacket."

Her attention was caught. She gave me a penetrating look. "Black?" What's happened, Celo? Tell me the truth!"

"Kamagore's dead."

She stared at me mutely for a while. I understood the reason for her silence. She was trying to make out whether I was telling the truth. She was the only one who knew that I had a reason to kill him. She had heard the curses I had directed at him from the impenetrable solitary confinement cell in Leopoldov prison which I had not stuck my nose out of for two years. "Poor Kamagore," she eventually said quietly with sincere sympathy. "He's brought you nothing but bad luck. Even so, I'm sorry for him," she added compassionately.

Her compassion was sincere. From what I had told her, she knew Kamagore almost as well as I did. She took a grey shirt out of the cupboard and a blue tie with inconspicuous pale blue stripes. She had better taste than I did. Thirty years working in a clothes factory had helped to refine her taste. It was thanks to her I had my job. She had chased away the clouds gathering over me, when I'd been sitting helplessly on the station platform. She had just casually mentioned that there was a vacancy for an assistant storeman where she worked.

"I doubt whether it's me they've been waiting for."

"I'll ask. I'll come and tell you tomorrow."

The next day she did indeed come to our house.

"They'll take you," she told me.

"Did you tell them where I've been and what I am?"

"Yes, I did. You're to show up at the factory tomorrow. The pay's not much good. I'm sorry I couldn't find you anything better."

"That doesn't matter!" I exclaimed. I was determined and willing to do anything, even for a meagre wage.

"I haven't been baking. I've got nothing to offer you," my mother apologised.

"Don't worry about that. Anyway, I must hurry off to help Mum in the field."

I went to see her out. We stood for a while in front of the house. People cast curious glances in our direction. The village would have something to talk about. "Have you heard? Young Bizub and Opatovský's girl."

My mother, however, was ahead of them all.

"A good girl, that Milka Opatovská," she remarked thoughtfully. "She's the one you should marry."

I stared at her open-mouthed. And then burst out laughing, until tears ran down my cheeks.

Our wedding was in sixty-one, just after the New Year. After twenty-eight years of marriage little has changed in our relationship. Even now, when she was standing with her back to me and taking the shirt and tie from the cupboard, I unwittingly noticed that her hips were still like a girl's, as if she had never given birth. And when she turned round, the nipples of her firm breasts were outlined under her beige blouse with its round collar. If those outside had not been waiting for me, I would have pulled her down on the sofa and, filled with desire, I would have unbuttoned her blouse and kissed her breasts, while she silently stroked my head. We hadn't had sex for over a week. Then we would have lain beside each other, the reflected light from the dark green beet fields merging with the moonlight and flowing over our naked bodies like a warm waterfall. The night wind would have tangled itself in the curtains and hissed like a harmless, inquisitive snake. We would have stood together in the bathroom, gazing at our equally aging faces, with differently placed wrinkles on our foreheads and next to our eyes.

My sudden departure worried her even more than she let herself show. She was afraid for me. I wasn't happy about it either, but I couldn't add my anxiety to hers. The thought of looking into the face of a dead person horrified me.

I got dressed, kissed Milka on the cheek and went out into the yard, then into the street. It was quiet and still basking in the May sun. The white church rose on top of the green hill and on the surface of the river the dark contours of the coming night were already settling.

Few people would believe me if I said that in the comfortable interior of the alabaster white limousine I did not reflect on the past. The Almighty is a spendthrift. He has provided people with a large number of special trains and whole sets of carriages, operated by blind and dumb engine drivers and train guards. The furnishings of the different carriages are of varied quality and range from plush seats to wooden benches, from heated compartments to ones with frost-covered windows. The pleasant company of kind and willing people to talk to alternates with that of robbers and hired killers, prostitutes and homosexuals. Night and day, seasons, stations and countries all follow in turn. You are a passenger without knowing the station which the guard will tell you to get off at. Everything is prison, life included.

When on that occasion years and years ago they pulled me out of the black saloon in the prison yard, they blindfolded me with some kind of rag. That was the beginning of the game of blind man's bluff. If we were more observant, we would realise that this children's game was invented by life itself. Nowadays it would not surprise me as much as it did then. Apart from that, they strip you naked, make you feel ashamed; they deprive you of the remains of your shell, cocoon, tinfoil; they expose your core, your essence; they degrade your ego in your own eyes. You become a mouse surrounded by enemies.

There were five of us boys returning home from church along the road. On the way we caught sight of a little grey mouse—a field mouse—at the bottom of a freshly-dug ditch. The sides of the ditch were not yet covered with grass; they were smooth and slippery after the night's rain. A puddle glimmered in the bottom.

"Ah-ha, lads, a mouse!" cried Martin Moško.

The field mouse was crouching stock-still at the bottom of the ditch. We surrounded it on all sides and then let out a terrific yell. The mouse took fright and tried to escape. But we didn't allow it to climb out of the ditch; we kept chasing it back to the bottom. It scampered from one end to the next and each time it involuntarily bathed in the puddle. We thought this hilarious. We didn't feel the slightest bit sorry for it. It was only laughter that brought tears to our eyes. At the same time we were in the grip of grim excitement. We realised that the life or death of this tiny, insignificant creature was in our hands.

How many times did that mouse run the endless distance between life and death? Fifty, a hundred? I don't know. Maybe when it ran into that puddle for the hundredth-and-first time it didn't run out of it; it remained lying in it, its terrified gaze taking us in for one second more, its tiny legs quivering and stiffening once and for all.

I remembered it that night when the interrogator came for me. He led me blindfolded along smooth, cold corridors. In his office he took the towel off my eyes, pointed to the wooden triangle built into the corner of the room and allowed me to sit down on it. He himself sat down at the desk and turned on the table lamp. Its light fell on a typewriter, green like the army uniform, and then it lit up my face, rousing me from my drowsy state. It was midnight, maybe a few minutes after, and I was not used to staying up at night.

"Do you know why you are here, Mr Bizub?"

"No, I don't. It's probably a mistake." I was once again thinking they'd confused me with my father. Why else would they dignify me with the title of "Mr"? I must admit it was a silly idea. The age difference between me and my father was too great to be overlooked. But I couldn't think of any other explanation.

"We're not mistaken, Mr Bizub." "I haven't done anything."

"Really?" The interrogator got up from his desk and took a couple of steps in my direction. He was a tall, slim thirty-five to forty-year old of darkish complexion and his uniform fitted him perfectly. He stared at me for several minutes without saying anything. I had the feeling that he was examining my insides, that he was trying to peer into my brain, search my genes. He finally had enough of looking at me, turned on his heel and once more sat down at his typewriter. He put a sheet of paper in the machine and began to type, while reading aloud what he had written, "The accused Bizub states the following about his criminal activities..."

"Accused? Criminal activities?" It was the first time in my life I had come across these words. I didn't understand a thing. I had found myself in a foreign land; some native was talking to me in an unknown language. I was sorry I didn't understand him. Maybe he needed help but I could be of no assistance. I shrugged my shoulders helplessly. I felt that something inside me, my subconscious perhaps, was longing for an explanation, a clarification of the circumstances, even the revelation of some offence I had unwittingly committed. Knowing my offence would perhaps help me to achieve forgiveness, then everything would at last be clear to me, leaving a great silence around and in me. "And I can't remember any more sins," I would say humbly, hanging my head.

"I took you for a sensible boy, Mr Bizub," said the interrogator after a moment's silence. "After all, you attended grammar school." He knitted his eyebrows and pursed his lips, thus making clear his sincere disappointment with my intellectual or moral failure. "What did your teachers teach you there? Did you know Mr Krčík?"

I brightened up. At last a question I understood. The ground felt firmer under my feet. I'd be sure to get out of this quagmire onto dry land very soon. Krčík was an excellent teacher. He had us for physics.

"Only for physics?" the older man smiled ironically.

"In the third year," I added this information.

"What sort of relationship did you have?"

"Just a normal one."

"What do you mean by normal?"

"Well... good," I explained, uncertainly.

"Did you visit Mr Krčík in his flat in St. Ann's Square?"

"Yes."

"When was that?"

"In spring. Sometime in May."

"Were you alone or was there someone else?"

"A classmate."

"His name!"

"Egon. Egon Singer."

"What did you do there?"

"Nothing. We sat." We had met at Krčík's place in the late afternoon. He had invited us. Then we really had sat and listened to the radio. Miro Jablonský was to have come too, but he didn't. Someone had died in his family and he'd had to go to the funeral.

The interrogator pinned me down with a black look. When he broke the silence, his voice reflected not only disappointment, but also sorrow.

"You can't just have sat there. You must have done something else. So come on, remember."

"We listened to the radio." And not only that. We admired it. That was because Mr Krčík had designed and constructed it himself. Egon, Miro and I were mad about electrical engineering. I can still see that radio. It was a beautiful light brown box with rather deep acoustics. But more than the resistors, coils and valves, I was fascinated by the lit up frequency dial with the names of radio stations printed in black. Paris. London. Moscow. Rome. Prague. Bratislava. In those names I could see the world, cities at night, millions of shining lamps; I heard the call of faraway places, the sweet tones of serenades and sonatas, words, most of which I did not understand.

"A radio? Wasn't it a transmitter by any chance?"

"A radio."

"Are you sure?"

"Of course," I said boldly, although I had never seen a transmitter in my life.

The interrogator tilted his head back. He looked as if he needed to release some pressure in his head. Suddenly he returned to his original position. He stared at me with visible disgust. He wrinkled his nose and his nostrils quivered.

"Stop putting on this act, Bizub!" he shouted at me. "In your own interests tell the truth. I have information that that Jew took advantage of you not only politically, but also sexually."

I had clearly moved into another galaxy. I floundered about in nebulae astronomers had no idea existed.

"I presume you know at least that Mr Krčík's original name was Feldmann? When we searched his flat we found the components necessary for constructing a transmitter. Mr Krčík was an agent of the Israeli Secret Service. It's time you realised, Bizub, that you were assisting a spy!" The officer yelled as if he had just been waiting all this time for an opportunity to let off steam. His black looks intensified and faded like a glow discharge tube. All my thoughts sank into the quagmire, plunged into the mist. Suddenly I was someone else. Something in my life ceased to add up. A couple of links had fallen out of the chain and I couldn't find them. I discovered in myself a vast emptiness. I had become outer space.

"Don't pretend to be more stupid than you really are, Bizub. You don't mean to claim that you know nothing about Krčík and Singer leaving the republic illegally."

Did I know? Didn't I know? I had registered the fact that neither of them had appeared at school after the holidays. There was some rumour they had taken flight, but no one had officially confirmed it, or denied it either. Then it dawned on me! I was there in their place! It was four o'clock in the morning. When would it begin to get light? I sat in the corner of the office on the wooden triangle like a heap of misery. Someone knocked on the door.

"Come in!" yelled the interrogator. A prison warder entered.

"Take him away!"

The screw blindfolded me with a towel and led me back to my cell. I couldn't lie down because he didn't unlock and let down the folding wall bed. An hour later the interrogator came for me again. With a towel covering my eyes he pushed me forwards and backwards, stopped me and ordered me to go on walking, like an elephant in a circus. I was dead tired. Once in his office, I automatically collapsed on the wooden triangle in the corner.

"Stand to attention, Bizub, and report," said the interrogator coldly. His tone catapulted me out of my seat.

"Report?"

"Detainee number 110 reports."

In a very feeble voice I reported and slumped down on the life-saving triangle.

"From now on you will report like that each time. Is that clear?" I nodded. "Sit down." He began to rummage in some documents. At the same time, he addressed me sweetly: "How are you, Mr Bizub?"

"Fine," I mumbled.

"How come you're fine?"

"Just am." I kept yawning every few seconds.

"You want to sleep."

"Really badly."

"If you tell me all about your criminal activities, I'll arrange for them to let you sleep until lunchtime."

"I'm not guilty. I haven't done anything. I'm innocent! Why don't you believe me?"

I had clearly antagonised the interrogator once and for all, which is why he again called in the screw and had him take me back to my cell. Days and weeks passed without him remembering me. For weeks on end I roamed around that cell. It was the longest journey in my life with all the attendant characteristics. Sometimes I was climbing upwards, but then I was slipping down and falling into the abyss before pulling myself out of it. At times this was accompanied by the feeling that I was not alive, that I was dead. The relief I felt at that thought seemed to confirm it. Something inside me really did die; my connection with the world, with people, with myself was broken off. Every day I descended into my abyss; I got used to it like an animal to its den. One morning outside the frosted wired glass window I caught sight of fluttering wings. A second later I realised they were snowflakes. Snow was falling, snowflakes were sticking to the glass of the barred windows; they were peeping inside and to me they looked like the eyes of inquisitive angels. The sky was full of angel wings. And I would have liked to turn into an angel and fly over the land, but my feet dragged me down; they didn't let down the folding chair and as I had nowhere to sit I crouched in the corner of the cell and instead of breathing out I forced a whisper through my cracked lips:

I'm innocent. I'm innocent. The guard would bang three times on the metal door. I got to my feet again and continued my endless march. This went on for days and weeks until I felt that my angel wings had fallen off on the way and that my innocence was beginning to rot and stink like carrion. I hurled myself at the door, filled with fear that no one would hear me; with all my strength I banged on it with my fists and kicked it with my feet. When the keys jangled in the seven locks and the door opened at last, I threw myself into the guard's arms and cried, "I want to testify. I'm innocent. Call the investigator. Take me to him. I'll tell you everything."

This abnormal era turned everything upside down. I was a little harmless mouse and yet someone—God perhaps?—had picked me out from among thousands, maybe millions of similar little creatures. But why had it been me he pointed at? I don't know. All kinds of things that at first glance seem senseless and without reason come to be explained one day; every puzzle gives up its secret. Maybe at the end of my life, in my last thought, I may succeed in drawing back the curtain, revealing the meaning of events shrouded in mystery and thus finally erase the anguish embittering my life to the last second. However, the fact that I was never proved guilty does not prove my innocence. To my death I shall pray for forgiveness of my sins. There is no difference between a mouse in a concrete cage and a real mouse in a ditch. We are all condemned to die. For this reason too the pipedream of life fascinates us with its seemingly easily attainable offer of better times. We try to improve our position, lighten our life's burden and win the favour of people we suppose can intercede for us with both the visible and invisible powers of the visible and invisible worlds.

They shoved that man into my cell some time after Christmas. I had the impression that the guard thrust him in with me against his will. He was a lanky, unshaven thirty-year old. The edges of his eyelids were inflamed. To me his arrival seemed like that of a swallow announcing the spring. His hands shook. His nerves must have been stretched to breaking point. Or he had not been allowed a wink of sleep for a couple of nights. We eyed each other distrustfully. He very quickly made himself at home in the cell, which seemed rather strange to me, but only until he confided to me in a whisper who he really was and what those there (he pointed scornfully towards the cell door) would never ever find out: an English spy.

"What will they do to you?" I asked, horrified.

"I won't confess to anything. After a few days they'll have to let me go." He must really have been sure of this, because he lit a cigarette and smoked unconcernedly.

"Have you been abroad?"

"Of course. I spent a year in America and two years in Britain. Those there," again he nodded in the direction of the door, "know absolutely nothing about that."

I admired his calm, the cunning way he had managed to slip out of the deadly trap. I was a little, inexperienced and trusting mouse in a concrete cage.

"What are you in here for?" he asked eventually.

I told him my story—non-story. He immediately offered me his services.

"They're bound to let me go. Don't you want to send a message to your family or someone else?"

"If you could tell my family not to worry about me."

"Of course. I'll call them from the station."

"We haven't got a telephone," I said ashamedly.

He was a little taken aback, but immediately came up with a solution. "Never mind. Give me the address. I'll write to them."

I told him my address. I was deeply touched by the idea that there was someone in the world willing to help me. My gratitude had no limits. I was determined to share the last crumb of bread with him, to give him even half my life. He could see it written on my face. He smiled at me. "You can rely on me," he said softly. "We spies are specially trained. Isn't there anything important you want me to tell someone? Someone who could be in danger because he was in contact with Mr Krčík? I might be able to help them. Arrange for them to escape over the border. Or at least warn them."

"Warn them? Against what?"

"Against being arrested. Or do you think they'll be satisfied with just you?"

Unfortunately, I remembered another teacher, Mr Kudla. He shared an office with Mr Krčík. They had been students together. They had had their weddings on the same day and been each other's best man. Apart from that, they had both been present when I happened to knock the bust of Generalissimo Stalin off a metal locker in the office when trying to open its jammed door. Although Mr Kudla did try to catch it, it slipped through his fingers and broke into little pieces.

Krčík had been the first to come to his senses.

"That could lead to trouble, Celo. Throw the bits into the bin and empty it into the dustbin. Make sure no one sees you do it!"

One dustbin stood in front of the school, another in the school yard. I chose the latter. Mr Kudla took an old newspaper and covered the contents of the bin with it.

"Mr Kudla!" I whispered.

I did not mention the broken bust to the spy.

"What about him?" he wanted to know.

"I think he should be careful."

"Did you say Kudla?"

"Kudla, Juraj."

"Okay. I'll warn him. I'll take care of him." In the evening the cell door was opened.

"Burda, take your things and come with me."

Burda smiled triumphantly. "Didn't I tell you they'd let me go?" He stuck his blanket under his arm, shook hands with me and was gone. I never saw or heard of him again. Only later, when I caught sight of Mr Kudla sitting next to me on the bench of the accused was the curtain whisked back and I saw my sin in all its nakedness. It hadn't even occurred to me that I had never mentioned Mr Krčík's name to my cellmate, so he had no way of finding out about him. And in spite of that he had said: "because he was in contact with Mr Krčík!" He was an agent provocateur. Who knows who he really was! He may in fact have been a spy, which might have cost him his head, so he had accepted this role from the all-powerful director. Maybe he had a wife and children at home and he wanted to buy off some of his guilt. He had played his role perfectly.

We passed the Tesla factory. The white building was basking in the afternoon sun. A little group of men and women in white coats were standing around in front of the entrance. Two men in dark suits got out of a silver-grey limousine. The older and shorter of the two was completely bald. With bitterness in my heart I remembered that I too had wanted to be an electrical engineer. Perhaps I would have been one of those who were now shaking hands with people from the ministry. But I didn't become an engineer; I didn't even have time to sit my school-leaving exams. I was hard put to manage that years later. While working I managed to complete a course at the electro-technical college. I studied of my own accord, without the permission and knowledge of the management, therefore I couldn't claim time off for study. I earned a little extra where and how I could. Saturdays and Sundays I went to unload railway waggons and two or three times a year I submitted a suggestion for some innovation. The last one earned me an audience with the chief power engineer. I had suggested a way to connect the factory's indoor and outdoor lighting to a photocell. This would save quite a few thousand every year.

"Come in, Mr Bizub," he welcomed me genially. "Thank you."

"Take a seat."

I sat down in the comfortable leather armchair and once more I didn't forget to thank him.

"Will you have coffee?"

"Yes, please."

"Evička, one coffee."

The secretary was a slim, long-legged blonde in tight black trousers and a red blouse. She put a cup of coffee in front of me with two lumps of sugar. She turned around in the doorway and smiled kindly at me.

"If you don't mind, Mr Bizub, we'll get down to business," said the boss.

"Please do."

"You submitted an interesting idea for innovation."

"I'm glad it interested you."

"However, your calculations seem a bit exaggerated."

"I can count," I objected. "I know how many lights there are in the courtyard and how many around the fence. And I know how much the factory pays for one kilowatt."

"I would suggest dividing the savings into two parts. That way our proposal would be more likely to be accepted by our company accountant."

"That's not possible," I remarked confidently.

"Then we would have to let him in on it too."

"Who?"

"The company accountant. But don't worry; we'd still get a nice sum of money out of it."

"In that case I'll take my innovation back."

For a while he played with the pencils and documents on his desk. Then he looked at me with narrowed eyes. He focused his gaze, searching for the weak spot I suppose every person has. He managed to find it fairly quickly.

"But, if I'm rightly informed, you have a prison record," he remarked with regret.

"I've done my time," I retorted sharply.

"And you have no professional training."

"I finished electro-technical college."

"But you work in the finished products store!" he objected in surprise.

"What's wrong with that?" I was tired, fed up; I'd had enough of interrogations and explanations. Whose business was it that I'd done time? Especially in the case of a thirty-five-year old who, in view of his and my age, should not belong to my group of persecutors and ill-wishers.

For a while he again played around with the pencils and papers on his desk. He made one telephone call. Then he looked at me conspiratorially. In a lowered voice he said, "I think I could do something for you."

"What do you have in mind, sir?"

"Wouldn't you like to work in supplies? You would be in charge of electrotechnical materials."

I rather liked the idea. I might get higher pay. I wouldn't have to earn extra by submitting innovations and unloading waggons on Saturdays and Sundays.

"If you're not afraid to give me such a job..." I indirectly agreed with obvious apprehension. But he did hesitate after all.

"Just a moment... In '68... Didn't you have some problems? Did the Commission screen you?"

"Manual workers weren't screened."

His face lit up. He was thinking of himself, not me. He didn't want to get into trouble. He had a wife and children too. No doubt they were better off than my wife and children. I was earning one thousand three hundred and Milka nine hundred after tax. We didn't even have enough over for a bottle of wine to celebrate a birthday or name day.

He looked at me in a noticeably kinder manner. I sensed we were nearer an agreement than a moment ago.

"So what shall we do with your innovation?"

"I'll leave that up to you, sir."

"You won't regret it. They won't rip me off so easily."

"I'll give you a free hand."

"I'll call you as soon as the management approves it."

"Thank you." I was already standing in the doorway and about to close the door from outside, when he called me back.

"That supplies job would only come into consideration in January next year."

"Okay," I said. "I'll hold out till then."

It was September. The swallows were gathering on the telegraph wires.

On the way we passed a small group of young hitch-hikers. Mostly girls. I hit the roof when my daughter once confessed she had hitch-hiked home. As if she didn't know how many perverts were watching for such an opportunity.

We were stopped by police on the motorway. Twice, in fact. The car had an ordinary number plate. In spite of the fact that both the secret policemen stuck their service cards under their colleagues' noses, they still looked into the car.

"What's going on?"

"An escape."

"How many?"

"Two."

"Where from?"

"Ilava prison."

I had to laugh to myself. Only a madman would run to the motorway and thumb a lift. No doubt they were crouching in the bushes along the river bank and would only continue their escape after dark. Or they would travel by goods train; sometimes it was possible to jump on one while it was moving. An escape is usually the culmination of long preparation and infinitely complicated deliberation. Maybe today's escapees are not patient and persistent enough. That's why most of them get caught after two or three days. The longest they manage to stay out is a week or two. They are usually caught at their girlfriend's house. The grapes of freedom hang up high. Only a few manage to win in the unequal struggle with the law.

The first chance I had in this regard was when they were taking me from Ilava to Pankrác.[7] The bus was dragging itself up the hairpin bends on the Moravian-Slovak border. There were about thirty of us prisoners, guarded by four men with machine guns. I was all skin and bone so the handcuffs were almost hanging off me. I cautiously tried to slip one hand out of the cold, shiny bracelet. I succeeded. I was more or less free. I only had to break the window, jump out of the crawling bus and run into the forest. I doubt whether they would have followed me. And if so, certainly not all four of them. After all, someone would have had to stay to guard the other prisoners. It was a mind-blowing thought. I almost stopped breathing. Suddenly I realised how knackered I was. I weighed fifty-two kilos. I wouldn't even have the strength to run. One guard would easily catch up with me. Perhaps if I was more desperate and longed to die, I would not respond to the command: Stop, or I'll shoot! And I'd let him kill me. The minutes piled up, one on top of another, ticking quietly within me. All of a sudden they were a huge obstacle. Meanwhile, the bus had clambered to the top and was now gathering speed downhill. The temptation was over. I submissively slipped my hand back in the cuff.

On one more occasion I spontaneously longed for freedom like this. I'd been behind bars for over fifteen months when my mother came to visit me. Dad didn't come with her; the train fare for two would have been terribly expensive. What's more, a visit like that took up three days. The hut for visits was five kilometres from the camp. The fencing there was much simpler than that around the camp. There were no guard

---

7   Ilava prison in Slovakia to Pankrác prison in Prague

towers, ditches, rolls of barbed wire. They used to take us there by bus with a couple of prison warders and several soldiers to guard us. It was in December, the visit before Christmas. When I got out of the bus the snow crunched under my feet. It smelled of whiteness and cleanness. Who knows why that smell reminded me of apples—I could never understand it. Nothing but snow all around: a huge white sheet, with the golden glow of the winter sun pouring over it. The sparkle of snowflakes sent an irresistible message into space which I could hear. I had an urge to run into the field, roll around in the snow. I felt suddenly hot. I flung out my arms and began to run. I ran round the bus and was about to do it again when one of the guards with a machine gun stood in my path.

"Stop! What are you doing?"

Others hurried to surround me and one of them handcuffed me. My euphoria evaporated quicker than mist and I came back down to earth with a hard bang. I sheepishly looked around at the faces of the armed guards, searching among them for one who would have zapped me without mercy. The wires of the fencing were sparkling with hoar frost. They led me back to the bus.

My visit was over. My mother saw me and, thinking they were going to shoot me, she burst into tears. It would be six weeks to the next visit. And Christmas was ruined. They only let me out of the punishment cell on Christmas Day. For a change, Father Josef and Kamagore found themselves there, the priest because he had served Midnight Mass on Christmas Eve. Although I hadn't been able to take part, I can well imagine that moment. Brabec had no doubt managed to swipe an extra bucket of coal. The fire in the stove would be flickering, the hands of the chess players motionless over the chessboard, while the others were sitting at the table, murmuring the words of the prayers with the priest. Kamagore would be lounging on his bed, his back turned to the whole world with a blanket pulled over his head; he even shut out the view from the window with its dark blue night sky studded with stars.

In his corner Father Josef is serving Mass. The lemon-yellow moonlight flows down his vestment—he is dressed in a nightshirt that reaches to his knees. He serves Mass every Sunday, but outdoors. The vault of the heavens is also the vault of God's temple. Only the initiated know this. It takes place during walks in the yard. Believers and non-believers walk in a circle around the hut. At that moment they are all children of God. Their humility is perceptible. Those who follow and understand Father Josef's gestures even pray along with him.

"Dominus vobiscum."

"Et cum spiritu tuo."

And how much more moving and powerful an experience must Midnight Mass be!

"And in the same region there were shepherds out in the fields keeping watch over their flock at night, when suddenly an angel of the Lord appeared before them, and the glory of the Lord shone around them, and they were very afraid. But the angel said to them: "Do not be afraid, for I have brought you good news of great joy, which will be for all people. For today in the city of David a Saviour has been born for you, who is Christ the Lord."

It was just as the host was being elevated that Človíček and his attendants entered the cell. The prisoners had vainly hoped that on Christmas Eve the screws would leave them in peace. They had also been so engrossed in the rite that all their senses and instincts were subordinated to this mysterious moment. Two guards remained in the doorway and Človíček stole up behind the priest. The outstretched arms of Father Josef, holding the host, dropped wearily to his sides. He turned to face the senior officer. For a few seconds the guard silently stared musingly into the eyes of the head shorter and twenty-five years older man, for whom after the war Pope Pius XII had sent a special plane to the concentration camp.

"Show me your hands!"

The priest lifts the hand holding the host to his mouth, places the wafer between his wrinkled lips and after a while swallows it.

Človíček grabs him by the neck, shakes him and yells: "What have you done? You've eaten it!"

"Yes, sir," the priest confesses meekly. "What was it?"

"The body of the Lord, sir."

"How did you come by it?"

"The Lord sent it to me."

"Who by? His name! I want to know his name!"

"It was an angel, sir. The Lord's angel."

Človíček thrust the priest aside. The bunk bed shook. "Search the cell!"

In the meantime some of those he had caught had lain down. Now the guards drove them out of bed and turned the room inside out. Everyone knew what they were looking for: wafers. But they didn't manage to find the treasure.

"You'll come with us," said Človíček to the priest for whom the Pope had sent a special plane to the concentration camp.

"Yes, officer," the most innocent of us all meekly replied.

"The rest of you—lie down!"

At that moment something happens which no one had expected. There is a crashing sound as Kamagore jumps from the upper bunk onto the floor. Človíček looks alarmed. When he catches sight of Kamagore he relaxes. "You're meant to be asleep, Hoffart!" he cautions him in an almost friendly tone.

"I forgot to pray before going to sleep, Officer," says Kamagore with a smile. And believe it or not, he kneels beside the bed and begins to say the Lord's Prayer out loud. He doesn't know the words; he gets it all mixed up; it is ridiculous and moving and still no one understands the meaning of this performance. Father Josef is standing next to Človíček, his head bent. He is praying with Kamagore, correcting his mistakes, so that his prayer will reach God in the true form.

Človíček at last draws aside the curtain.

"You soon won't feel like playing around, Hoffart. Put your shoes on!"

"If I must," Kamagore says with a smile. And he begins to get dressed and put his shoes on.

When they have left, those who remain crowd to the window and watch the dark silhouettes moving towards the gate; they hear the far-carrying crunching of the guards' boots in the hard-frozen snow.

"It must be terribly cold there," sighs Markovič.

"Twenty below zero at least," says Brabec expertly.

There is no heating in the punishment cell. Hoar frost is bristling like animal fur on the wires. Our room is growing cold too. All the coal has been used up. Brabec doesn't dare go out now to steal a bucket of coal from the enclosure. He doesn't want to end up in the punishment cell.

Yes, that bastard Kamagore was sometimes magnanimous, more so than I was; I, in my pettiness, was not able to see as far as his heights and perhaps it was just that feeling, the feeling of inferiority, that later led me to cling to a quiet, but unrelenting decades-long desire for revenge. I could not forgive him that wrong, which was not in fact his fault. All this could be seen in my eyes, it protruded from them, even shone like the snow on Mount Fuji. If I had caught sight of myself at that moment in the mirror, it would certainly have chilled my heart and my soul. It was a good thing the secret policeman didn't notice that hoarfrost. In the car it was dark, the engine purred monotonously and the policemen talked together about some football match, while I prepared to meet Kamagore once again.

I thought back to our meeting the week before with an anxiety I could not understand and a distaste that I could. I had already felt that anxiety in the bus on the way to Bratislava. It changed into a slight shiver that made me tremble like an aspen leaf in the breeze. Then it hit me perceptibly harder in the vestibule of the hotel in which Kamagore was staying. It knocked the breath out of me; I reeled and had to lean against a post supporting the studded brass banister. When the mists that had almost swallowed me had cleared, I staggered over to the reception desk. Meanwhile, I was vaguely aware of people moving around; lightly dressed guests, men and women, and liveried staff. One of the two receptionists gave me her attention. For one second her gaze was radiant and for the rest of the time it showed unconcealed indifference.

"Can I help you, sir?"

"I've come to see Mr Hoffart." Having been tense for so long, my vocal chords must have weakened, because that first time I didn't manage to produce a confident, clear and conclusive message.

The receptionist looked infinitely bored. "Who?"

"Mr Hoffart," I repeated slightly more confidently.

"That American?"

"Yes."

"I doubt whether he'll have time for you now," she remarked with obvious irony.

"He's expecting me. Could you please tell him that..."

The receptionist did not let me finish. She lifted the telephone receiver. "Who should I announce?"

"Bizub. Celo Bizub."

For a long time no one answered the phone. I sat down in a leather armchair. When I looked at the receptionist again she was just replacing the receiver. She must have spoken to Hoffart, because her charming lips passed on the message through the wide space of the hotel lobby: "Mr Hoffart will come immediately."

I looked towards the staircase; just below it the doors of the lift kept quietly opening and closing with a slight click. Young girls were coming down the stairs dressed like nymphs on seaside beaches. Blocking my view of the lift, however, was a huge banana plant. A fountain was bubbling pleasantly beside it. The brass statue of a girl bathing was beginning to acquire a patina. Probably just at the moment when I was paying more attention to this bronze figure, the hotel lift stopped at the ground floor and a citizen of the United States of America, Peter Hoffart, stepped out. He had his arm around the shoulders of a long-legged and long-haired girl wearing a tight banana-coloured pullover and a denim miniskirt. But my attention was only for the silver-haired gentleman in a blue jacket and light grey trousers, with gold-rimmed glasses, who was patting her round behind. You old son of a bitch, I thought to myself. Then I saw them stop at the reception desk. The receptionist prodded the air with her finger in my direction; the man turned round and yelled for everyone in the hall to hear, "Kamagore!"

I would never have dreamed that that old womanizer was my best and, in fact, only buddy. It can't be Kamagore, I thought, feeling bewildered. The picture I saw in no way corresponded with the picture whose authenticity I could have confirmed. I didn't have time to sort out in my head all the possibilities and impossibilities arising from this, because I would have had to run through the events of whole decades step by step, page by page. I got to my feet and Hoffart hurried over to me, as if he just couldn't wait to meet me and all the way he was bawling, "Celo, old buddy! Celo, you old bugger! Celo, you moron!" I recognised that voice, that yelling immediately. Once again it filled me with disgust and sadness. That disgust and sadness must have appeared in my eyes, or in some grimace on my face, because when he was only a few paces from me, Kamagore suddenly hesitated and halted. Then he looked round. "Darling. We'll see each other later," he said to the girl he had left at the reception desk. Thanks to that, we were both given time to overcome the infinite distance between us. Not only the splashing of water could be heard, but also the grinding of the jaws of time, which calmly and unhurriedly, with the routine of a pathologist, was working in the bowels of our unrecognisably changed bodily frames. Life is the greatest enemy of life. It is our own personal prisoner and that is why it works against us. It gnaws away at us from the moment of conception; it ravages us internally and externally and the moment it bites its way through us to freedom, it kills us without mercy.

"Hello, Kamagore," I whispered quietly.

The tension, uncertainty and curiosity in his face relaxed, but he didn't move from the spot. He probably guessed that I had not yet got over the painful joy of our meeting, nor overcome the embarrassment of an uneasy conscience. Or he saw in my eyes the snow that fell almost without stopping in February 1956. In spite of this, he attempted a smile. It didn't come out well. I took it to be a smirk and it scared me. I felt I had caught a glimpse of his soul through a crack in his eyes. And then black sludge came rushing from my soul. I was struck dumb and blinded; I found myself under a landslide. Through the silence and darkness I invisibly fought my way back to the light so I could see this buddy who years ago had thrust me out of his life. It was an undeserved punishment.

By '56 I had done three years of my time, which was a sixth of the sentence I'd been given. The rest—fifteen years—hung over me like Damocles' sword. It might not chop my head off, but it could wipe it clean like the censor could a newspaper. For some people this would be deliverance: they would forget where they had come from and where they wanted to get to. They would not remember the name of the woman who had given birth to them, and they would confuse the name of their father with the name of the ex officio defence lawyer. I did not intend to finish like that. I did not want to end up like Jožko Michalko, whose will was broken in the interrogation room. He had been serving in the border guards' unit and had apparently tried to escape abroad. When at last they sentenced him and took him off to the camp, he did not even notice that he was now in a space much bigger than his cell. In spite of that, they sent him down the mines to clean out the gullies. He spent whole mornings or afternoons marching around the room, but although he walked round the table like a hungry man around hot porridge, he was not going in circles. His was an incomprehensibly dogged and inhumanly silent struggle to force his way through the dense undergrowth of his waning awareness towards the light at the end of the tunnel. Outwardly it was like a real march, with turns to the left and right, as well as about turns; with this military drill Jožko was turning the ground under his feet into increasingly heavy ploughed soil, onto which he would one day drop, never to rise again.

I think it was at the end of November; it was snowing for the first time that winter and Kamagore and I were standing next to each other for the evening roll call. The watchtowers and the camp were shrouded in a thin curtain of falling snow; the floodlights and camp lights beyond it winked at us like wolves' eyes surrounding the black huddle of prisoners. The bales of barbed wire that stretched between the huts like fat pigs were disappearing under the snow. These were the first obstacle for any escapee; there he would probably give up wanting to compete with the law. At the same time, the snow touched up the photograph of the landscape, smoothing out the bumps, softening the rough parts, playing down and hiding the dangerous ones.

The evening roll call took longer than usual. Probably the numbers didn't tally or the guards were drawing it out on purpose, so that the two thousand convicts could taste to the full the charms of the coming winter. My feet were beginning to go numb with cold. And not only mine. Several people were vigorously stamping their feet, the damp foot-rags in their work shoes or rubber boots no longer providing warmth; just then those who had stuffed their footwear with old newspapers were best off.

Kamagore watched with lively interest the snowflakes that were falling to the ground in graceful arcs. At one moment he leaned towards me and whispered: "If we ran away now, no one would even notice."

"A brilliant idea," I said ironically.

"You're not up for it?"

"No," I retorted. "Suicide's not for me."

"You'll snuff it anyway." Kamagore objected.

"Hope dies last."

"That's what cowards say."

"I'm not a coward. I don't want to die. I want to live a bit longer."

"You call this living?" he muttered scornfully.

I looked at him. In his eyes I saw black tar melting and seeping down to somewhere in the depths of his soul. It was clear to me that he had been toying with the idea of escaping for some time. For me at that moment the thought that I could be free was about as real as the idea of life after death. To go against the wire and the snipers in the watchtowers into no man's land was to go to certain death.

"It'd work," said Kamagore, as if he had been reading my thoughts.

"You're crazy!" I whispered, although I had a strong urge to yell it at the top of my voice. But we were surrounded by a sea of human beings who had eyes and, above all, ears. If someone who shouldn't overheard our conversation and reported it to the authorities, we would both be dealt two or three years extra. Fortunately the screws eventually managed to match the number of convicts in the camp with the list of those sent to the pits and a senior officer ordered the men back to their huts. That was the end of our discussion, because shortly afterwards the loudspeakers announced the line-up for supper. And two hours later the roll call for the night shift. I was on that shift and so was Kamagore.

I used to work on the excavator with a tall, flabby teacher. He was doing time for sexually abusing his pupils. I found him so repulsive that I often didn't exchange a word with him the whole night. Kamagore was better off. He worked on the surface with the waggons carrying waste rock onto the slag heap. King Kamagore had his seat on that hill. There he could converse with the wind and the sun, the birds and the clouds, the stars and the moon, with the lead and silver that over thousands of years had turned into uranium. The slag heap was an ever-hungry prehistoric lizard;

day after day generations of miners brought it bloodless stone sacrifices and from time to time a bloody sacrifice too. Only this enabled it to grow higher and higher every year. It grew fast and over the years it had become an excellent lookout. Kamagore must have felt that he could see the whole world from there, the nearby railway and the stream winding along beside it, rising with it into the pine wood. It was from here that the insistent call of the cuckoo reached Kamagore's ears every spring.

All that night, even when I was drilling holes into the rock, I could not shake off the delusionary dream Kamagore had shared with me. Two thoughts competed in my mind for dubious priority: the first, that I would lose my life trying to escape; the second, that I would spend the next sixteen years in this hole in the company of creatures like my present companion—a bugger of a teacher.

Both were a nightmare. The worst thing was that I couldn't confide my dream to anyone. So I floundered about alone in my thoughts. What was more precious: freedom or life? Milanovič had waited almost eight months for death in a death cell and still he longed for life. Early in the morning, the keys scraped in the lock of his cell, he never knew whether he was being taken to his death or for a walk. Suddenly I remembered the words of the teacher Markovič. "The classical writer who advises us that it is better not to be than to be a slave, is not right. We mustn't take poetry literally. The written word is just a feeble gesture of immortal genius in the bloodstream of mortals." These words could decide my dispute with Kamagore. And once, it seemed to me, they did decide it.

When I left the pit it was still dark, as if morning was only a continuation of night. The darkness was slowly retreating and the guard towers and camp huts emerging from it like sleeping giants and whale backs. I handed in my carbide lamp. Kamagore was waiting for me there. He grinned, his eyes shone; he didn't know what to do with his hands and feet, his nerves were so tense.

"I've swiped some wire cutters," he boasted, when he had at last calmed down a bit. That was great news, but even so I couldn't resist a scoffing remark.

"Are you hiding them under your coat by any chance?" With my right hand I made as if I really did want to draw back the long warm coat we'd been issued for the winter.

He took a step back. "Don't you believe me?"

"It's all the same to me. I won't be going with you anyway," I declared outright.

"Pity," he retorted with unconcealed sadness in his voice.

For two months we left each other in peace.

After travelling for an hour, I'd had quite enough of the car. I began to feel my back, my old problem. I can't sit for long, especially in one place and one position. Not even the thought of what was awaiting me in half an hour or so, something I wanted to get over and done with as soon as possible, could inspire me much to put up with it. I would have liked best to give up on it all, dead Kamagore included. But that wasn't possible. Without me, without my testimony, they wouldn't bury him. Flooded in golden light, the road was going directly towards the sun. In this situation who would want to think about a dead body? My companions chatted away about all kinds of things, anything but the case they were clearly working on. Or did they want to drive me prematurely out of my hiding place? Because at one point in the middle of a quiet conversation about some league football match, the detective inserted a question: "There's one thing I don't understand, Mr Bizub."

"What's that?"

"Why it was you that Hoffart remembered. After all, you weren't the only person in this country doing time with him."

"He's the one who could answer that best, don't you think?"

"He's dead. Someone murdered him," the secret policeman reminded me ominously.

"I only know that from you. But I don't know the answer to your question."

"You don't know, or you don't want to know?"

The question remained hanging in the air for several seconds like a storm cloud. And it was clear to me that rain would fall from it.

"I haven't got anything to hide, gentlemen," I said calmly.

"But you have, Bizub."

At that moment I understood something. Something I could have realised when I caught sight of these two in my yard. *They suspect me! They want to provoke me!* flashed through my mind. Uncover me like a potato pit. In the cold winter of life I may have frozen to the extent that rot was now destroying me. In their silent expectancy I could see a clear challenge: Come on, Bizub, show us your frostbite, your anxiety and fear. And your guilt.

It was time to go on the offensive. But I did nothing. My strength left me. I realised there was no point. They know about her. About the girl in Kamagore's hotel suite. She was not the same one he had his arm around at the reception desk. That one came back accompanied by a waitress and potboy and one more important waiter, maybe the head waiter. They pushed three trolleys heaped with bottles and food into the suite. My eyes goggled at this undoubtedly expensive load. I could only distinguish the bottles of champagne from the other bottles and three platters of food heavy with all kinds of goodies I couldn't put a name to.

"Your order, Mr Hoffart," said the head waiter grandly and respectfully at the same time.

The hotel staff quietly disappeared from the room. And I still couldn't bring myself to sit down in the deep armchair upholstered in dark blue velvet with a touch of purple. Underneath a gold framed mirror was a little white table and on it an obviously expensive vase of Carlsbad glass. Holding an enormous bouquet of yellow tulips, it looked like a plump matron. There were eye-catching black, yellow and blue triangles, rectangles and diamond shapes in the grey carpet. I stood on one spot and revolved around my axis like the Earth. I was quite bowled over by this splendour and extravagance.

Then the bedroom door opened and a girl came out. When I saw her, the first thing I realised was my own scruffiness. I stared at her as if she was the embodiment of a dream. To this day I think I might only have dreamt her up. She was wearing a flimsy flowered dress with a deep neckline. Her curly dark chestnut hair rested on her shoulders. Her eyes were, I think, green and they sparkled like pure snow in the sunshine. I looked at Hoffart. He gazed back at me with an ungrudging, benevolent smile. That smile said: this girl is a gift from me, Celo. Take her.

At last I sat down. The girl stood in front of me. She smelled like an exotic rose. I've never ever smelt such a perfume. With the help of that, I could sniff her out even in a smoggy town. She smiled at me.

"I'm Melita. And you?"

I was ashamed to tell her my name. I'd had no practice with such a situation. "Call me old man," I said.

She stroked my cheek. "As you wish, old man."

I felt myself blushing. Kamagore laughed his raucous laugh, the same I'd heard when he'd spoken to me on the phone. It sent shivers down my spine. The curtains in the room were drawn. In the pleasant semi-darkness I noticed Kamagore's sunken cheeks, tired eyes and the gold pin dividing a red tie with lots of white dots. And the gold signet ring on the middle finger of his right hand. And the gold watch on his left wrist, and the bracelet of yellow metal. And I noticed one more thing: the invisible seal of loneliness clearly stamped on his every gesture, in the way he walked, even in the movement of his eyelids. He sprawled out on the wide sofa. The girl in the miniskirt and banana-yellow pullover sat down next to him.

He leaned towards me and quietly asked what I thought of the girls.

"You haven't changed a bit," I said.

"No, I haven't changed. We only live once, don't we?" he said with a laugh.

"You're still the same old pig."

"Help yourself." He somehow sensed I had a strong urge to insult him. "You can sock me one and I won't be the slightest bit angry with you."

"Maybe I will," I said. The girl next to me shrank away apprehensively. Then she had an idea. Her eyes lit up like emeralds. She took one of the three bottles of champagne out of the ice bucket, deftly opened it and poured the wine into the glasses. It was a pale pink.

"There, that's a good idea!" Kamagore said appreciatively. He lifted his glass, directed a meaningful look at me and smiled. "To our meeting, Celo."

"Cheers," I said. We clinked glasses. We drank. Breathed in and out. The time had come to open the textbook of our private history and turn to a certain chapter in it.

"Tell me then!" Kamagore invited me. "You first!"

We asked each other almost exactly the same questions. "Are you married? Have you got any children? What did you do and what are you doing?" I learned that in America Kamagore had got married. His wife was a divorcee, the owner of a motel and mother of a six-year-old boy. He had lived with them for twenty-two years. Six years ago they had both been killed in a car accident. He was now rich. He lived in a twelve-room house somewhere near Boston. However, we tiptoed around one question, the most important one, as if it were a sleeping princess. It wasn't good manners to bother strangers with the greatest event in our lives.

We ate and drank, drank and ate. In between we danced with the girls to music from a tape recorder.

It was spring. Outside the trees were in blossom, pink and white petals were floating in the air like fluffy feathers. Everything was easy, sweet, bearable, but all at once a picture of still, gloomy-green beet fields imposed itself on this scene and I awoke with a start from my dream and the gentle petals of dying blossom suddenly became real snowflakes.

The snow was tumbling down on the rocky landscape like an act of God. It seemed as if even the slag heaps were sagging under the burden, but at the same time it gave people the feeling that the camp huts were cosier and the ground under their feet warmer. However, it was a hard job getting to the mines. In the barbed-wire corridor connecting the camp to the pit the snow was over our knees.

It was the beginning of a new year. I learned from the camp radio that I was allowed a visit. That gave me a fresh appetite for life and dispelled my dirty mood. The previous one that hadn't taken place had filled my mother with fears for me and at the same time, with an unprecedented rush of energy, she had set to writing applications and chasing up all kinds of certificates, all so they would allow her another visit. At the end of January it worked out at last. She received permission to visit me. She came with Aunt Mária, Dad's sister. For most of the time she said nothing, but her eyes clung to me and there was the same expression on her face that I had seen when they sentenced me. She had been sitting in the first row, just behind the bench for the accused. This privilege was given to the mothers and wives of all those accused. I turned round several times and smiled at her to reassure her. In contrast to the other wives and mothers, she did not cry. In her eyes there was a look of amazement similar to that when you catch sight of a picture you have seen before, but only in a dream.

Later she told me of a dream she had had a few weeks before I was arrested. In that dream two men had come to see her in the field. She was digging potatoes. "What do you want?" she had asked. "We've come to tell you that your only son will die," they said. It was like passing a sentence. She was horrified. She threw herself on her knees and begged the two to let me live. Her pleas and laments eventually softened them. They looked at each other and both nodded.

"But he will suffer a lot," said one of them at length. They left immediately, but somehow too quickly, as if they had melted into the horizon, so they didn't hear my mother cry out, "Suffer? Why? Why?"

A secret had entered her life; a secret she could not share with anyone, least of all with me.

Her loving heart was not spared suffering even on the above-mentioned visit. It wasn't she who profited from her hard-won victory, but someone very different, a stranger called Emília, the sister of my fellow prisoner Hieronym. During a visit the convicts sat on one side of a wide table, relatives on the other. Hieronym and I lived in the same hut, and now we were sitting next to each other, so I could not help seeing his sister, a nineteenyear-old beauty with a heavy fair plait down her back, big blue eyes, a wide face and a fascinating voice that in my ears very nearly became a song. We couldn't keep our eyes off each other. My aunt noticed, but she didn't say anything, she just smiled indulgently. A bit later my mother noticed too. Then I glimpsed a little cloud of displeasure on her forehead. Who knows what thought had crossed her mind? She may have realised that sooner or later another woman would steal her son. But really, she must have been aware that for the time being no such danger threatened either me or her. Nevertheless, that girl turned my life upside down. I fell in love with her at first sight. My eyes and ears were full of her. A bullet-proof wall of light radiating from that girl separated me from my mother and aunt. The visit came to an end and instead of my mother and aunt I said goodbye in my heart to her, a stranger, a girl I had not even held hands with. Then I included trite verses in my friend's letters, thoughts taken from books I was reading and greetings, thus stealing two or three lines from the thirty we were allowed to write once a month to our closest relatives. But that wasn't everything. It was then that I came to fully realise my position. I was almost twenty-three and I had the prospect of another thirteen years in prison. That girl would never be mine. I would never embrace my first love, nor would I kiss her.

One day she would stop adding lines for me to the letters she addressed to her brother, because she would want to marry a young man who could kiss and embrace her. Or I would be transferred to a different camp and that would be the end of it all for both of us. Then I realised how ridiculous were these naïve little verses and other inventive greetings included in Hieronym's letters.

You must break free! Run away! my mind cried.

It was time to speak to Kamagore about this. During the evening roll call I asked him whether he had anything against my breaking out with him, or whether in the meantime he had found someone else to join him and had lost interest in me.

"I've got a partner," he grunted.

Serves me right, I shouldn't have dithered, I thought bitterly. It ruined the whole evening for me. I was furious with myself. That evening, when cleaning my teeth in the washroom, my mood unexpectedly changed. Kamagore was washing next to me and I noticed that he was physically much fitter than I was. His bulging arm and leg muscles were clearly the result of everyday exertion. "Hey, I can hardly recognise you," I said with undisguised admiration. Kamagore shrugged his shoulders.

"You see."

"How do you do it? Weight-lifting or what?"

"You try running up the slag heap thirty times a shift and smashing twenty boulders with a hammer and you'll be the same."

"You do all that? Why?"

"To be fit."

I had not expected Kamagore would be able to focus himself like that. Subconsciously I, who liked him, had the same opinion of him as those who underestimated him. And the result? While I was dillydallying at the crossroads, he was already on his way along the straight road to the wide open spaces. That's the end of it, I thought. I suddenly felt dead tired. I was like someone under a death sentence who had just been told that the president had turned down his plea for mercy. "When are you going?" I asked Kamagore without being in the least interested and feeling very low in spirits.

"When the weather's right."

"You've got a partner. So we'll be saying goodbye," I muttered more to myself than to him.

"I have, but he's useless. He'll only be a nuisance."

"Then don't take him!" I exclaimed.

"I can't bring it off by myself."

"I'll go with you."

"You'll change your mind at the last moment," he commented, looking me straight in the eye. We saw each other then as never before: clearly and in detail like under a magnifying glass—for both the first and the last time in our lives. At that moment we were alone in the world. We had no parents, country, past or way out. We had no choice. We had to take up the challenge we had set ourselves. We had to trust one another.

And then came the evening when heavy snow clouds rolled across the moon and snow began to tumble down on the landscape once more. It was a Monday, we had had risotto for supper and I thought I'd had enough, but Kamagore drew me outside, saying we'd try and scrounge seconds from the cook. For half a mess tin of rice in which it was a real miracle to find a scrap of meat, it was hardly worth the effort. But I let myself be persuaded. The moon kept surfacing from the clouds like a drowning man from a river. It lit up and darkened the quiet landscape and urged me to sleep, to calmly enjoy the silence. The snow beneath our feet was fragrant and yielding. The whitened space around the still, black huts, the moon fleeing from the embrace of the rushing clouds and we two with clanging aluminium mess tins in our hands—that was in fact the first sequence of the film that would be shown that evening. Kamagore, that is, as soon as he had breathed in that incredible almost Christmassy atmosphere, looked up at the sky and around him and suddenly murmured, "I'm going!"

"Where do you want to go?" I hadn't understood.
"Today or never."
"What do you want to do?" I still had no idea.
"I'll eat. I'll get dressed before nine," he spoke as if he was talking to himself. "I'll go out. If the men ask, I'll tell them I've changed shifts, that I'm going on the night shift. You'll go a quarter of an hour later as if you're going out for a breath of fresh air. We'll meet between the kitchen and the store."

At last it dawned on me. I really had been very slow on the uptake. The surprise knocked the breath out of me. I barely managed to stutter a couple of words: "Today? Now? In this weather? You're crazy!"

I shall never forget the look Kamagore gave me.

"Have you shit yourself?"

"No, but..." I was shaking like a leaf. My heart was jumping because I couldn't catch my breath. Snowflakes were sticking to my face. They fluttered around the lamps and spotlights on the poles in the fencing and on the watchtowers. Frost on the barbed wire bristled like the fur of an enraged beast of prey. Horrible snow! Foul winter! Cursed labour camp!

Kamagore was clearly thinking about my words. After a moment's consideration, he came to a decision: "Okay. I didn't say anything. Let's go—to get that second helping."

I was relieved. We went to get that crappy risotto. And then we returned to the hut.

The gentlemen with whom I had the honour of travelling in the alabaster-white Tatra 613 limousine did not show any inclination to run over the snow-covered plains of my life with me. That did not interest them. To my surprise, they knew far too much of my antics in the hotel suite, especially about the fight that broke out a few minutes after midnight between Kamagore and me. I know that these sentences will provoke an indulgent grin on the reader's face. What could two men over sixty be fighting over? Surely not the two whores keeping them company? It's a good thing Milka didn't see me. Making a fool of myself like that towards the end of my life!

We ate and drank, drank and ate.

Kamagore asked me, "Did you ever imagine that we would sit and wine and dine like this together?"

"Not even in my dreams," I said truthfully.

"Have you ever eaten caviar? Drunk French cognac?"

"No, never so much as wanted to."

"There was a time when we even liked risotto, wasn't there?"

"We had no choice."

"And when I was on the run, I caught a rabbit and gutted it with a piece of broken branch and lived off it for two days. My stomach turns to think of it even now." His mouth was smiling, but his nose was wrinkled in disgust.

"Mine too," I said impatiently.

"And that margarine! D'you remember how we shovelled it in?" His face was burning, memories lighting it up like candles in a cemetery. His whole being was immersed in them and only certain parts of his body obtruded—the hands he gutted the rabbit with, the feet that had carried him far away from the accomplice he had deserted outside the gate of life. He noticed I was watching him. He gave me a sad, diffident old man's smile. That ripped apart the mist of drunkenness that had for a time protected him from me.

The royal feast was just reaching its climax. From this height, as if from the top of a real hill, I unintentionally caught a glimpse of myself as if in a mirror. I was pathetic! I was overcome with shame and at the same time filled with unimaginable fury. The girls were giggling. Kamagore started playing a game of forfeits with them using an empty bottle of champagne. However, at the critical moment the girls demanded an extra fee: a hundred dollars. Only then did I learn that they would each be getting a hundred dollars for spending the night with us. Apart from that, another hundred was needed to bribe the receptionist and someone else, probably a policeman. That was too much for me. What's more, I am not used to alcohol: the wine, cocktails, cognac, undiluted whisky and who knows what other alcoholic miracles were bound to knock me out.

In the middle of the wildest revels, I grabbed the tape recorder, lifted it above my head and roaring like a wounded animal, smashed it to bits against the arm of the sofa.

Then the film came to a halt.

Kamagore stopped shaking his head; the half-naked girls froze open-mouthed to the spot where they were standing—on the table. And my aching spirit was like a pressure cooker: "Kamagore! What have you done to me? Is this what you called me here for? I've got a wife and children. That's all I've got in this world. You haven't got anyone. Wasn't once enough for you to trick and betray me? Do you want me to lose everything I have? You're pathetic."

"Why do you put all the blame on me? I left you because you couldn't go on."

"I only sprained my ankle, that's all!" I cried. "It swelled up a bit and you took advantage of the situation and bolted."

"You couldn't even step on that foot, you couldn't pull your boot on, it was freezing, how did you expect to go on? Barefoot?" Kamagore argued calmly, convincingly.

"You said we were only one night away from the border; I could have made it," I shouted.

Kamagore was smiling all the time. That made me go berserk. I smashed his smile with my fist. Then once again and again and yet again. I have never fought with anyone in my life. He fell to the floor and remained lying on his back on the carpet. I threw myself on him again and I banged his head on the floor until the girls managed to pull me off him. He didn't defend himself at all. It was a moving and mortifying performance.

"Kill me," he said suddenly.

"You've been dead for ages," I said callously. "For me you died the moment you ditched me."

"So why did you come?"

"To kill you," I declared, full of furious and genuine hatred that in my alcoholic madness flared up like a haystack.

One of the girls picked up the telephone and began dialling, when Kamagore calmly said, "Don't call anyone. This is our problem. Don't interfere, darling."

It had all happened like in a bad film.

I could see these scenes, because I experienced them for myself.

When the call came to line up for the night shift, Kamagore got ready as if he was on it: he put on his long coat, wound his foot rags round his feet, lined his wellington boots with old newspapers, clapped his cap on his head, muttered something and left the room. I hurried out after him. There wasn't a soul in the corridor yet, apart from Beladič, of course, who was on duty in the hut then and whose job it was to go round the rooms alerting people. Everyone left for the night shift at the last moment, each wanting to make the most of that last second of the quiet, peaceful evening. I only caught up with Kamagore beside the desk of the man on duty.

"Where are you going, Kamagore?"

"I'm on the night shift," he grunted.

"That's a lie!" I exclaimed.

"What do you want me to tell you?"

"The truth."

"What use would that be to you? You'd better sneak back into the room, so you don't get into trouble because of me," he said almost in a whisper, looking round nervously.

"You want to escape in this bad weather?" I asked him, this time taking more care.

"It's precisely this weather that suits me."

"You're crazy."

"Think what you like," and he abruptly turned away from me.

"Kamagore!" I called quietly. But by then I was staring at his back. He was moving away from me and I thought it would be forever. He didn't look round, but went out into the night, falling into it as into a snowdrift. I ran after him and hissed in his ear: "Wait. Don't leave me here. I'm going with you."

But he didn't stop even then. He just said curtly over his shoulder, "I'll wait for you behind the kitchen. Wrap up well. Be sure not to forget your gloves."

"Gloves? I haven't got any," I groaned.

"Work gloves," he snapped without so much as glancing at me and seeing my anxiety or commiserating with my wretchedness.

Back in the room I had the feeling that no one had registered his departure. I slipped out of the room in the same manner. Or did I? In such situations the rule is not to see or hear anything; to be blind and deaf. Later, when called one by one to the commander's office and questioned about Kamagore and me, asked whether they had noticed anything, whether we had shown any sign, had let anything slip, in short whether they had been aware that we were preparing to escape, they could all to the last man truthfully reply that they had not heard anything, not seen anything nor noticed anything suspicious.

So, nothing suspicious happened in the room, and at work? How could they notice anything when we were working in different places? They denied knowledge of us, it is true, but not like Peter, when he denied knowing his Master. They were in fact placing us under their protection. However that escape fascinated everyone and the occupants of the room accordingly corrected their opinion of Hoffart. In short, they kept their fingers crossed for us and I could imagine Father Josef praying for us every evening, "Let us pray for two of our brothers who need God's help now more than ever."

Heavy snow clouds raced across the sky; the black huddle of the night shift was getting ready to roll out of the main gate. The shift leader was going through the lists, reading names, and the prisoners were passing one by one through the main gate towards the gate into the barbed-wire corridor, arranging themselves in rows of five, with the guards standing at the sides and in front; everything was going smoothly, that is, like on a hundred, three hundred, six hundred and maybe even a thousand evenings before; a tiresome routine for both guards and prisoners alike, nothing more, until the moment when flares blazed over the camp, flooding the whole area with brilliant blue, yellow and white light, to be immediately followed by the sound of shooting. About that time we were already through the first wire fence. Kamagore was right in thinking that when the night shift was getting ready, the attention of the screws and the guards in the towers would be focused on what was going on around the gate. We had easily managed to throw over the barbed wire a plank that had been lying for ages under the snow beside the wall of the neighbouring hut. We ran over it into the sniper zone. There we lay down and on my left side I held a hastily constructed shield: a blanket stretched across a wooden frame. Kamagore had wound a blanket around his body, while the frame and wire cutters had been hidden under a pile of coal in the enclosure behind the kitchen. He cut through the second wire fence, while I swiftly stretched the wires apart, enlarging the hole to make it easier and quicker to pull ourselves through into the open corridor. So far everything had gone as planned, we had gained a few precious minutes, but when we were crawling through the most dangerous section of the corridor, the guards in the towers caught sight of us and began shooting.

By that time the camp was astir. Those who were sitting at tables and playing chess or drinking tea, as well as those who were already lying in their beds in warm rooms, hurriedly got dressed, put their shoes on and ran out with a feeling of dread, glancing at each other: WHO? At that time only Kamagore and I knew the answer to that question. It would take several precious minutes before the camp was surrounded by troops and filled with guards armed with machine guns, driving the prisoners back from the courtyard to their beds in their rooms and turning out the lights.

Kamagore set to cutting through the second strip of barbed wire fencing; I helped by widening the gap in the wire netting with one hand, while using the other to hold the frame with the taut blanket that was protecting us from the bullets. We were lying on the frozen ground, pressed into the snow and I was shaking violently, but not from the cold; from time to time I felt terribly hot, but my teeth would not stop chattering. I noticed a bullet had dug itself into the ground a little way in front of me and that brought me to my senses, so I stopped waving the shield like a fan and I tilted it as Kamagore had strictly instructed me to do. However, I still don't know whether the taut blanket really did deflect the bullets, whether hitting it really did make them change direction.

To me, all this seemed to take an eternity. When I rolled over on my side a piece of wire jabbed my right foot and I thought it was a bullet, that in a minute I would get one in the head and that would be the end of me. For the first time I realized my life was in danger. My arms and legs were suddenly heavy and once we were on the other side of the netting I felt sick and almost vomited, but then I heard the barking of dogs and I forgot about the pain and nausea, my fear of dying, the anguish of living, my parents and that girl, my friends, in short about everything, and I ran after Hoffart; we zigzagged through the trees like shadows, running like hell, because then it was not a question of freedom, but of life and death.

The siren was still wailing, the dogs barking, the flares did not disappear from the sky.

Kamagore looked round. "The stream! The stream!" he called to me, pointing to somewhere ahead in the darkness broken with little specks of snowy light.

At the end of the wood surrounding the camp there was a stream. We would be wading in its wintry waters until dawn. Good God, I only hope my wellingtons haven't got holes! I thought to myself when I eventually stepped into it.

We ran on without stopping, the barking of the dogs and the commands of their handlers gradually fading into silence; only the flares continued to blaze for a long time in the invisible sky, slowly dying out halfway back to earth. Just before dawn, still running, or rather stumbling, we reached the spot where the stream flowed into the river. We hid under an iron bridge connecting the banks of this river, whose name we did not know; with the last of our strength we pulled ourselves up into the steel structure of the bridge and there we nested like birds on a wide sheet of metal, on which we found a couple of cement bags and piles of bird droppings. We each ate a square of chocolate, which Kamagore said he had received before Christmas from a doorkeeper—a civilian employee—an old woman who was crazy about him and we broke off a chunk of bread he had swiped from the camp kitchen, covered ourselves with the blanket I had carried wound round my body and we fell into a deep sleep.

In that hotel suite Kamagore, looking all in, picked himself up from the carpet with a lot of help from the girls, while I went down in his place like a freshly felled tree. The floor revolved with me, everything around me kept disappearing and reappearing from somewhere; I was swimming backstroke, trying in vain with outstretched arms to hold back or at least change the direction of the current that was carrying me away to an unknown destination; then I was suddenly whirling on a merry-go-round that someone had lifted me onto. For a while I resisted the temptation to close my eyes; I tried to keep them open and go on seeing, but in vain; I kept falling asleep and waking up. Meanwhile I could hear Kamagore's wheezy laughter; I felt someone pressing a glass to my lips with something aromatic and sticky and then I fell asleep for good.

I woke up in the middle of the night. I was lying on the bed stripped naked and next to me, wrapped in a light duvet, slept the girl whose rare name—Melita—I had difficulty in remembering. I quietly and stealthily began to get dressed, but only managed to pull on my boxer shorts and shirt before I felt sick and had to run to the toilet. Kamagore was lying in the other room on a pulled-out sofa; the girl resting at his side was completely naked, not entirely covered with a sheet and with her back to me. I must then have spent over half an hour in the loo and bathroom before I managed to rid myself of the heaviness that was weighing on my body and soul.

Then I noiselessly returned to the bedroom, finished getting dressed and without saying goodbye, tiptoed out of the suite. The young lady at the reception desk registered my flight from the bowels of the hotel with an understanding smile and a sweet, "Goodbye, sir." Cracks of daylight were already opening in the misty black clouds of the night; the fragrant air and whistling of the blackbirds eased the burden of sadness and shame that I was about to carry away with me from the city I sincerely hated, although it had clearly become involved in my unhappy fate only by chance, through no fault of its own. I slowly trudged through its deserted streets to the station. I bought a ticket, went out onto the platform and turned my life over in my mind like a coin that had long ceased to be valid. What had it all been about? Which side was heads and which tails? Not that I was so very dissatisfied with it, but I couldn't shake off the feeling that it was not the life I should have lived, that it was someone else's life, a stranger's, as if it were possible to switch lives like babies in a maternity hospital. And perhaps the person who should have had my life was no longer alive, while I was dipping my head into the fresh breeze blowing through the wind tunnel of the station. And when I stretched myself to straighten my back, which was aching from sitting too long and sleeping in an uncomfortable position, I beheld Kamagore standing before me. But I wasn't the least surprised to see him, which is why I didn't ask who had woken him, and whether he had only pretended to be asleep when I stole out of the room. I had guessed that our story could not remain half told.

"Here you are!" he cried with the relief of someone who after years of searching has found the human being he has been missing most.

"What do you want?" I muttered wearily, because with Kamagore's arrival I was overburdened by a fresh wave of deadly fatigue. "We two are through with each other."

"We really can't say goodbye like this."

"Then let's not say goodbye."

He misunderstood these words, which is why he caught at them like a drowning man at a straw. He considered them to be a call for reconciliation.

"Let me invite you and your wife to California. We'll lounge around on the ocean shore. We'll travel all over America. You'll have the holiday of your life. I'll buy you a car."

"You can stuff it now."

"You can't forgive me, can you?" he said, disappointed and taken aback.

I shook my head. "I tried to, but I can't."

"I've got no one but you in the world," he said, like a child who has just lost his father. He looked at me and there was so much loneliness in his eyes that I felt awful. Tiny beads of sweat were running slowly down his temples to his smooth-shaven cheeks. He took off his glasses and cleaned them with his handkerchief. He gazed at me and moved his lips; he clearly wanted to say something more, a word, a sentence, something you're allowed to say only once in a lifetime. But that little word could not find its way through his tightly-pressed lips. Then the invisible measure that is in every person was filled. The measure of love, pain, suffering, fear, cowardice, light and darkness.

His head fell to his chest; he turned on his heel, quickly ran down the stairs, for a while his footsteps echoed in the subway and then once again I only heard the blowing of the wind and saw the pink flower of dawn opening. A light gust of cool air brushed against me, searchingly stroking my face, maybe trying to discover whether I was awake or dreaming, and only a long time after did I realize that it was the angel of death.

A morgue is not a place one would visit if one didn't have to. If a cemetery is a final resting place, then this is a visiting room, where Kamagore received his last visit in this world. A permit for it was issued for my two companions plus one, that is me, all three by virtue of office. They showed it to an employee, who nodded to acknowledge he had seen us and that paper. He was tall, slim, young, bored, careworn, dressed all in white; I can't remember anything about his face, maybe because when a few minutes later Kamagore's oblong, bloodless face slipped out from under the sheet, all other faces lost their significance for me; the whole capacity of my memory was overloaded by this large detail, which stretched itself out in it like an unwelcome guest on a comfortable sofa. It would silently watch me, mock and feel sorry for me, get in the way, awaken me from my sleep, lie down in bed between me and Milka.

"Do you know this man, Mr Bizub?"

"Yes, I know him."

"What's his name?"

"Peter Hoffart."

"Thank you. We'll write the report in our office. You can cover him up," the captain told the employee. Through a window or door the sun managed to smuggle a single ray of light into the cold room. It flew around for a moment, hovering for a second over the motionless body; finally it hit a cold, snow-white tile with unexpected force and silently slipped down to the rough greywhite floor, where it died. Someone may have looked at their watch, or pushed against a glass door, or a woman taken a mirror out of her handbag to look at herself. But it is quite possible that it was Kamagore's soul that had come to say farewell to me, the large detail of his pointed face being replaced by another one.

At that time we were on the run for three days and four nights. We knew that by then the search for us had no doubt spread throughout the whole country, so in the daytime we didn't stick our noses out of the hiding place we had chosen before dawn. It was February, we didn't have much choice and we tried to guess what our pursuers would be thinking. We spent the first two days and nights relatively comfortably, because we were making our way along the river at night and spending the days above it in the structure of bridges, on metal platforms lined with the feathers and droppings of birds and the cement bags that Kamagore carried under his shirt. I had the blanket wound around my body and we used it to cover ourselves. We slept soundly, sleep making up for the loss of strength and the shortage of food. On the third night, however, we had to make up our minds whether to continue southwards or to turn west. We decided on the southern route. We left the river and its pleasant babble was replaced by the whoosh of the wind traversing the rugged plains and the dry crackling of branches in the forest. The sky cleared, it stopped snowing and grew colder; the wind blew the snow, covering our tracks. The night, or rather the early morning, brought us to a village of some kind. We went to within a stone's throw of it, came across a barn which was easier to get inside than into the kingdom of heaven. And when we were burying ourselves in the straw, we discovered a treasure trove in the form of eight hen's eggs. We silently blessed the hen and begged forgiveness of the farmer's wife who had not discovered where her hen had laid its eggs. We gulped down four eggs at once and kept the others for later. The fourth night sealed my fate: I sprained my right ankle on the uneven, hard-frozen ground. We slept in a hayloft that I had still managed to reach. Late in the afternoon we woke up, peered through the hay to scan the terrain and decided the coast was clear, so we could relieve ourselves, but when I tried to put on my boots, I cried out in pain.

"What's the matter?" Kamagore asked in alarm.

"Nothing. Nothing. Just that foot," I said.

"Does it hurt?"

"A bit."

"Show me!" Kamagore examined my painful ankle. It was swollen and all kinds of colours and when he poked his pointed fingers into it, it hurt, as if it was not just a sprain, but an open fracture. "That's bad," he muttered. "With a foot like that you haven't got a chance."

I felt my heart stop. "What chance? What d'you mean?"" In his eyes, in the wrinkles around them I caught a second's deliberation, after which he pronounced his verdict.

"You can't go any farther." It was a final decision. Irrevocable. And, above all, unjust. When he had passed sentence, he crawled out of the hay and then—as if nothing had happened—he went to relieve himself. I followed his example. I had only one boot on. I stood on one foot, leaning against the barn; I urinated into the virgin snow and when I was fastening my trousers, I lost my balance for a second and had to stand on both feet. I cried out in pain and toppled to the ground. Kamagore stood over me, legs apart like a champion winner over his defeated opponent. He stared down at me from a great height and I had the unmistakeable feeling that he was no longer seeing me; he did not want to see or hear me. The evening was nigh and as soon as the stars came out it would be time to set off. According to Kamagore, we were only a night's walk from the border zone. "Go and lie down. I'll try to find something to eat," he said. I kept my eyes fixed on him. I noticed he didn't even look at me.

"You want to slip away without me, don't you," I attacked.

At last he looked at me. His eyes were at once sympathetic, ashamed and icy. "I've no alternative. You wouldn't get there," he said.

I had to defend myself against his sympathy, as well as the shame of his suspicion that I could go no further. "I can walk! Look!" I took a couple of steps, but I almost blacked out and again howled in pain.

He supported me by the arm as I hopped around. "Don't kid yourself. You wouldn't get far. You must face up to it. Now it's sink or swim. So far it's been a long walk—now it will be a fight of man against man. Don't worry—I won't leave you without help." He reached into in his shirt and pulled out a piece of chocolate. "Here you are. I hid it for a rainy day. I was afraid from the very beginning that it would end up like this."

I refused the proffered alms, the payoff that Kamagore offered for breaking free of me. I looked around me. I heard the wind. The dark silhouette of the sparse forest reminded me of a pack of wolves. We were surrounded. Very soon even the stars would change into the luminous eyes of beasts of prey. *We won't survive!* flashed through my mind. Paradoxically, that calmed me. I went to lie down. He stayed on watch. He managed to catch a hungry, unwary rabbit. We had supper. It was like a sacrificial rite. The bloody sacrifice, however, divided us even more. Neither of us said a word during supper. Meanwhile, the darkness fell outside. I waited to see what would happen. I saw Kamagore wind the rags around his feet, pull on his boots and wrap the blanket around his body. The paper sacks he left for me. He pulled on his gloves and I realised that this was the end of our brotherhood. The definite end. I no longer cared.

"Go to the devil! Bugger off! I don't want to see you! You're a bastard! A rat! Is that what you do to a mate? I'd never do such a foul thing to you. I'd carry you on my back even to the end of the world," I jabbered with tears in my eyes.

He slid down from the hayloft, but he didn't leave me; he stood in front of me, his face close to mine, eye to eye, mouth to mouth, I could have poked his eyes out, pulled his tongue from his throat, but instead I slid down the hay to him, to his feet, I hugged them, held them with all my strength. I once more allowed him to look down on me from above, to feel like a conqueror. All it needed was one magnanimous gesture and he could have lifted me from his plinth onto his pedestal, and instead of the snowy dust of the ground I could have rested on the soft, warm bed of my monarchical friend. The night was lit up by the silvery shine of the snow; the silent stars and forest wolf pack watched us. It was the most beautiful of all evenings. I rested my face on his feet, whined like an animal, gripped his legs below his knees, jerked his body and he fell, toppling over me, thus freeing his legs from my arms, freeing himself from me; he jumped to his feet and when I crawled over to him, he kicked me away like a poisonous snake. However, I didn't stop crawling and reaching out for the toes of his boots, and he kept moving away from me. "Be sensible. We wouldn't get anywhere together. Don't you get it? It's for your own good. They won't catch me alive. But you've got a chance to survive. Maybe it'll be better for you like that. I couldn't bear to think you'd died because of me. Like this you'll stay alive. Be sensible, Celo. Don't make it even more difficult for me than it already is."

But he quickly realised that he was wasting his time with me; he reached into his shirt, took out a piece of bread with those squares of chocolate and threw it all in my face; he whirled around like an animal scared to death and dashed off into the wood, soaking into the snow like a dark stain, until he was nothing but darkness.

"You bastard!" I called after him. "Where are you running to? They'll kill you. Come back!" But I knew he would not. He had fled because he was afraid of me, although in fact he was scared of himself, scared that he would give in to my pleas, take pity on me and stay with me to the inevitable end.

I no longer cared about anything. I crawled up into the hayloft. For three days and four nights Kamagore's presence had protected me from fear and panic. Now that I was by myself, I was overcome by a dread of loneliness and helplessness. My teeth chattered; in panic I dug myself deeper and deeper into the hay, until I reached last year's damp grass and once more I dragged myself up so I could see the stars in the sky and a deer that fled when it caught wind of me. Every rustle, every crack of a branch or flapping of wings scared me out of my wits. When my anxiety overflowed its banks, I burst into tears like a child and howled like a wolf; fortunately the hay subdued me, numbed my pain, lulled my consciousness and I gratefully allowed myself to be bribed by sleep, that cheap substitute for life.

It was an uneasy sleep, but even so I wasn't fully awake until I heard the barking of dogs and a sharp command: "Hey, you there! You're surrounded. Give yourself up. Come out with your hands above your head. No nonsense."

I was gripped by terror. Through an opening in the hay I saw soldiers with machine guns and dogs at their heels. Of course I couldn't see all of them, but the hayloft was probably surrounded, and even if it hadn't been, there was no point in staying in my hiding place.

"Hey, you there! Did you hear what I said?"

I crawled out of my hiding place on all fours, falling to the ground head first and I didn't even have time to recover before a soldier was standing beside me with a machine gun aimed at my head. Others rushed over to me; they put handcuffs on my wrists, seized me under the armpits and by the collar and dragged me to another hayloft, behind which the officer in charge was standing. He took two photographs from his pocket, looked at me and muttered through tight lips, "That's Bizub. There's one more there." He left me lying face down on the ground.

"There's no one there," I spoke up.

"You're lying. Begin shooting and then release the dogs!"

While they were shooting I kept turning my head from side to side, pressing first one, then the other ear to the ground in order not to hear the shots. I felt they were shooting at me and that for some reason they couldn't quite finish me off. I began coughing, the whole of my body jumped up and down on the frozen ground. All this time the officer stood in front of me and didn't take his eyes off me. The dogs showed no interest in the hayloft. To make sure, the soldiers scattered the hay in the hope of finding the other one—Hoffart. But all they found was the empty cement bags.

"Where is he?" asked the officer.

"I don't know." My foot hurt me terribly.

"Which way did he run?"

"I don't know." My teeth were chattering.

They took me to the town, interrogated me, took down my statement, which I "read, agreed to and signed," handed me over to the court, which sentenced me to three years and dispatched me to the solitary confinement cells in Leopoldov prison.

And now I found myself once more where I had been years ago; I was again sitting in an investigating officer's office and through the open, but barred window came the twitter of swallows, the clatter and ringing of trams; I signed with my own hand the declaration that the dead body found exactly a week earlier in the passage under the square known as *Mierové námestie*, was that of Peter Hoffart, born May 16, 1929 in Bratislava, a US citizen, and I drank the coffee they offered me. Then they wrote down my statement in which I answered their questions about when, where and under what circumstances I had come to know Hoffmann, when and where we had met and what we'd settled at our last meeting in Bratislava. I was waiting for them to ask me why I had killed him, but that question did not come up. It had been too brutal a murder, six stab wounds in the chest and back, of which four were enough to kill him.

"There were at least two of them. Each wound was made with a different sharp instrument. He didn't suffer long," the detective commented encouragingly.

Less than an hour later I was already sitting on the station platform, the same one where early in the morning a week before Kamagore had come to beg me to forgive him. If I had done so, maybe I would have managed to keep the chalice of death away from his lips.

I arrived home before midnight and immediately went to lie down. The bed seemed to be lined with snow and ice. I only calmed down and warmed up when through the open window I caught a glimpse of the gloomy green of the beet fields. The moon was shining and the leaves glimmered in its light. My wife propped herself up on her elbow and fixed her eyes on me. After a while she overcame her diffidence, bent over me and kissed me on the mouth. The curtain moved in the light breeze and there was a rustling of the wings of the angel of love.

"Darling," Milka said to me. "Stop tormenting yourself. After all, you didn't kill him."

But I had my own ideas. The die was cast. The cup was full. I would never be wholly and finally forgiven.

I heard it when the wind got up. I imagined the grass in the wind. What else was my life but mown grass? The wind is a careless haymaker; it mindlessly shakes up the grass, throwing to the right what grew on the left and into the shade what grew in the sun. The next day the haymaker will come again and toss the left to the right and the right to the left. On the third day it will come for the last time and gather the hay into piles, all of which will smell equally sweet and sour. There will be grass in them from all corners of the world and each flower from a different place. For the life of one man is the life of all men and the life of all is also the life of a single man.

Forgive me, dear, don't ask me anything, don't want anything of me, let me rest. Tomorrow I must get up early in time to see the dew drying on the gloomy green of the beet leaves.

POEMS BY RUDOLF DOBIÁŠ

A LONG NIGHT'S STORIES

UNSENT LETTER

With my own cross in one cold cell
and far from Heaven indeed,
I wrote home: I feel very well,
there's nothing that I need.

The guardians guard me watchfully,
what can I have to dread?
I know God's mills are grinding me
and turning me to bread.

My body now so fever-bright
is God's own burning coal,
and these four walls of purest white
exalt Him and extol.

Mama, I'm feeling fine. It's true,
but I'm sad not to be with you.

*(from the collection Bells and Graves,
in the section Events from the Dusk)*

THE WIND IN MID-NOVEMBER

...

In mid-November
A wind wet as the footcloths
In torn gumboots just after surfacing
Sure to freeze instantly to the bone
And break off bits from toes
As if it were a small thing
To hop on one leg to the camp infirmary

...

Warm wind in mid-November
May it cover my comrades, Lord
Let them lie in your lee
So the pursuers with loaded rifles
Cannot find them
And shoot them
Half a century later
In the warm wind in mid-November
May I never more have to hear
The crunch of snow under soldiers' boots
And the howls of dogs
In the warm wind in mid-November
Broken in on by my silent howling

(an extract from a poem in the collection Between Grass and Wind. Poems from a Future Legacy, in the section The Four Seasons)

A LONG NIGHT'S STORIES

WHERE ARE YOU OFF TO, MEN OF JÁCHYMOV?
(AFTER ŠTEFAN PAULÍNY)

> Where are you off to, men of Jáchymov?
> Will you go down the mine to seek the ore?
> After so many years and so much weeping,
> back at the bottom, will you drudge once more?
>
> Where are you off to, men of Jáchymov?
> To be conveyed in cages, hang from ropes,
> and later, like a safety-pin, to fasten
> two praying hands with insubstantial hopes?
>
> Maybe your wish is, men of Jáchymov,
> to swing the heavy pick again till numb;
> seeking below the ground, though you see nothing,
> God's loving light in black uranium?
>
> Or will you venture, men of Jáchymov,
> to chase the trains you missed in times gone by,
> and afterwards, like birds when they're migrating,
> utter to all the passing winds your cry?
>
> Where are you off to, men of Jáchymov?
> Will you go down the mine to seek the ore,
> doing new tasks but in continued service,
> at your old calling as you were before?
>
> Tell me, please, tell me, men of Jáchymov:
> Who will remain for us when you're no more?
>
> *(from the collection Between Grass and Wind. Poems from a Future Legacy, in the section To Friends)*

YOUR LOVE

Your love comes on tiptoe
to my body
allergic to waking.
Old age has moved in there,
that tenant with lifelong title
and extravagant dreams
of a home of his own.

Your legs on high heels
rise from lowland to the summits
of my snowy peaks;
the chamois praise your poise,
leaping the abysses
gouged by Spring waters.

From the dust of my body
your assiduous hands
mix the warm clay of March,
where they sow appletrees
with fragile blossom,
lest my sweetness all be lost.

The wind tangles your hair,
like sea-waves, round my brow;
a net, where I am caught
like a careless whale.
You'll be the fisherwoman
who gives me life;

one day I'll repay you
with a peaceful death.

When parting time arrives
your love will come on tiptoe
to my mortal body,
check the rooms of my heart,
find a message in one,
written decades earlier,
take in ring-circled fingers,
read it, seal it with a kiss,
and like a fallen nestling
bury it beneath a shrine.

*(from the collection Between Grass and Wind.
Poems from a Future Legacy, in the section The Cold Dew)*

CONVERSATIONS WITH RÚT

Until now I thought you loved me,
with love for me you sleep and wake.
In our world, though, nothing's certain.
Life is only a ruthless press
grinding you when you've not yet ripened,
and grain and chaff alike are lost.

The tree's connected with each leaf;
certainty hangs on the uncertain;
and thus we two are close together.
We've become circles on the lake
where the white goose may wash her wings,
so they'll be clean to fly the heights.

If only we were in those circles,
and going to sleep you had my kiss,
and what's remote were by our side!
If only God in Heaven noticed
that I'm with you, you stand by me:
how nicely we grow old together!

(from the collection Conversations with Rút)

THE WOMAN WAITING

She waited. And he did not come.
Turbid rivers swept him from her.
There was no time for lamentations.
Too little strength remained for life.
In muteness she passed through the pain.
Sought solitude, there to be mute.
Meanwhile the wolfpack out of doors
at all the crossroads stood on guard.

In the apocalyptic story,
resembling very much despair,
only history's limping feet,
stumbling towards a dawning day,
encouraged her to hope for justice.

But that was nothing for a woman
carrying life at every step,
the under-apron fruit, the apple.
Day sat by day and year by year.
Everyone peeped through her window:
had any end come to her waiting?
And she was almost happy when
a courier with a letter from him
came to her house out past the shore.

Day sat by day and year by year.
And she sat often by the window,
in case he turned the curving roadway,
arriving home from his long journey.

He came, when trees had lost their blossom,
in May, as she stood on the porch.
The sun, surveying all the vineyards,
was hanging from the spider-webs.
Her man, always her child, had come,
returned to her alive and guiltless.
Slipped through the casemates and the fetters.

Seven long years I waited for him.
Whispered, My son. She'd no more strength.

Alive, though, she'd awaited him.

*(a poem from 1960 included in the collection
Conversations with Rút, in the section From a Chronicle)*

HOME

What's that pleasant smell?
Like we knew at home.
The sweet smell of bread,
that's the smell of home.

What's that pleasant smell
that home knows so well?
Home's eternal part,
like Mama's sweet heart.

What's that pleasant smell?
Like... it was at home.
Quenches thirst, provides...
That's the smell of home.

(from the collection Wind in a Hat)

THE HEART

It did not weep, it wept,
in stone it graved a song,
thankful for little things
and beating in the breast.

It did not wait, it waited
for what had lived in vain
and for what persevered
and what expired too soon.

It did not kneel, it knelt,
when it desired reward,
in desperation dared
to bury the newborn.

It was not mute, it muted;
sheer wedge, it pierced the mouth,
lodged somewhere in the throat,
lacked music for a song.

It did not weep, it wept,
depending when and who,
blew snowdrifts on the grave
over which I mutely kneel.

(from the collection Celebrations of Spring)

MORNING

Impudent stillness everywhere.
No wind blowing, not a puff.
If someone gives the evil eye to you,
don't pay him back. You don't have breath enough.

Then, as she frees the window blind,
she'll say (the woman who loves you):
"Even the mourner wishes he were glad.
And he who loves, and promised, can stay true."

Milk-jug in hand, as if she'd made
a rhyme and she would pour that in.
And tenderly she lays it on your bed,
to dress you in it, and undress you then.

And in that (maybe conscious) fear,
in awe (you both have felt its might),
she's standing in a storm before the house.
Rain lashes her, but she's a beam of light.

And then she takes a mirror-shard:
believes it will postpone eternity
and fly up high, so she'll descend,
using her bits of wings that still may be.

And bitterness grew sweet in her with time.
Then from the hive she called to you outside.
She smiled, and she grew younger so.
She smiled, accordingly she cried.

(from the collection Celebrations of Spring)

FROM SPRING

I stand by an open window. Look! a bee
   flying out from a petal.
I wait to see if the fragrant rose
   petal will speak to me.
But the petal keeps silence. Only the bee
   from the petal flew up to me
and put on a sweet manner as she pierced me
   with her sting.

AFTERWORD

RUDOLF DOBIÁŠ—THE SLOVAK SOLZHENITSYN

RUDOLF DOBIÁŠ (29. 9. 1934) is an author whose life and work can, in the post-Communist world, be likened only to that of Alexander Solzhenitsyn. While the Soviet author spent eight years in a gulag, Dobiáš spent seven working in a uranium mine (1953-60). He was born in Dobrá near Trenčín, a small village now part of Trenčianska Teplá, and his whole life is linked to the historical town of Trenčín as well as with the nearby spa town of Trenčianske Teplice. He was from a poor peasant family and his upbringing was much influenced by the deep religious beliefs of his parents and their strong Christian principles. In 1945, as a ten-year old, he witnessed the arrival of Soviet forces on Slovak soil and saw how a young Russian soldier died with the name of his mother on his lips as he succumbed to his injuries. Despite that experience, however, Dobiáš was against the expansion of Communism into central Europe from the very start, mainly because of the danger of atheism being enforced in the country. After the war he became an active member of the *Junák* scouting organization, which had close ties with the Catholic Church. He remembers as a scout taking part in religious processions and at Easter standing on guard outside Christ's tomb in the church in Trenčianska Teplá. After the February coup in 1948, the Communists banned the organization and its members had to break the law if they wanted to continue with their activities. They called their new organization *Stráž ľudu* (The People's Guard) and their leader was one

Ján Huňa. This illegal group of young people continued the work started by the *Biela légia* (White Legion), which was also based in Trenčín and had many members who lost their lives or freedom in their struggle to resist Communism. These victims are a recurrent theme in the literary work of Rudolf Dobiáš though it was only after the fall of Communism that he could finally describe their tragic fates in full.

His literary output is much influenced by his experience of imprisonment. Dobiáš received an 18-year sentence for allegedly working with others in "engaging in the anti-state activities of preparing and distributing leaflets, of gathering weapons and of illegal assembly with the end purpose of bringing down the people's democratic administration and replacing it with a so-called Slovak state" (taken from his sentence). He had been arrested on December 23th 1953 in his garden in Dobrá—and thanks, in part to having been to pre-Christmas confession in Bratislava a few days earlier, was able to cope well with his arrest. Dobiáš was tried as a member of the illegal *Stráž ľudu* organization in a trial that began in August 11th 1954. Their primary activity was producing and distributing anti-Communist leaflets and Dobiáš faced a death sentence if it could be proved that he was the ideological leader of the organization. This was a very real threat as Ján Huňa had told the police, under duress perhaps, that Dobiáš was their leader. It should be added that it was Huňa who not only led the secret *Stráž ľudu* organization but also designed the leaflets which were the direct cause of Dobiáš' arrest. Together, between 1950 and 1952, the organization designed six different leaflets, producing approximately fifty copies of each. As Dobiáš lived in Trenčianska Teplá and went to school in Trenčín, he would leave leaflets on the train, around the municipal park and at the station's public toilets. In the end he avoided a death sentence, in part due to the death in 1953 of Stalin and the courts' subsequent reluctance to execute criminals at any opportunity. His was still a severe sentence, though: eighteen years' imprisonment, of which he served more than seven. He worked in the

AFTERWORD

notorious Jáchymov uranium mines where he became acquainted with such people as Eugen Löbel, Anton Srholec, Eman and Jano Zábrana and others. He was released following the issue of an amnesty to mark the 15th anniversary of the liberation of Czechoslovakia by the Soviet army. After his release, he was socially marginalized for many years and it was only after 1989 that he could freely write about his experience of the totalitarian regime.

A special place in his work is occupied by the *Biela légia*, especially the sentencing and execution of three members who were former students of the Trenčín *gymnázium* he attended: Anton Tunega (1927-1951), Albert Pučík (1921-1951) and Eduard Tesár (1922-1951). Another member who was also convicted and sentenced to ten years was Ferdinand Daučík, a football international and manager of ŠK Bratislava and later FC Barcelona who had managed to emigrate from the country before he was due to be imprisoned. He had played for Slávia Praha from 1935 and took part in two World Cup tournaments, the second of which was in 1938. After emigrating to Spain, he became manager of FC Barcelona, led them to two league titles and helped strengthen the tradition of this world famous club.

The *Biela légia* was a movement with a clear agenda and was given its name by a man called Vicen after February 1948, even though it had existed as an organization since 1945. Their aims were as follows: to resist Communism and its ideology; to uphold Christianity and the application of its values in both public and private life; to introduce a human social system in Slovakia; and to establish a genuinely democratic regime in Slovakia in accordance with the democratic principles declared by Pope Pius XII in his Christmas message of 1944.

The execution of the three former students is a recurrent theme artistically fictionalized in Dobiáš' work. One example of this is his chapter about the sentencing and execution of Tomáš Chovan (1926-1951), a lieutenant in the Czechoslovak People's Army. On the evening before his execution, his mother, brother Jozef and uncle came to say goodbye to him. The mother, writes the author: "...had to bring her son clothes the authorities would dress him in for his final journey. An hour later they could go and look at him. How surprised they were, though, to see a stranger in the clothes they had brought... And then Jozef Chovan found his brother's body" *Zvony a hroby (Bells and Graves)* (2000). The same motif of clothes being exchanged is used in the story *Mladší brat (Younger Brother)* and forms what is probably the most powerful part of the text. The narrator is the younger brother of the man executed and although he is still not fully grown up, he becomes an adult upon the execution of his brother: "The child in me died", says the narrator at the end of the story. The tale about the exchange of clothes, based on real events, is related by the younger brother in the following extract: "I saw him once more, lifeless in the mortuary. Three condemned men were executed that dreary morning. We had spent the night at the station and at six were already in the mortuary... Mama took my hand and led me to the open coffin. I saw the sharp profile of a man with a shaven head; his hands, sticking out from the black suit with its grey stripes, lay motionless on his chest. It was Tomáš' graduation suit. Only when we got closer did we notice that it was another, older, unknown man lying there in his suit". This story is one of Dobiáš' masterpieces, gives a true picture of the proletarian dictatorship in conditions specific to Czechoslovakia and reflects the imperialist tendencies sweeping through central Europe and originating in Moscow.

After the Second World War, several central European states fell under the influence of the Soviet Union and became so-called Socialist countries. Soviet pressure was such that although we did not become a part of the Soviet Union in the way countries like Estonia, Latvia, Lithuania and Armenia did, a certain colonial dependency arose which we could not escape from. In one of his famous essays, *The Abduction of the West* Milan Kundera wrote: *"The geography of Europe (extending from*

AFTERWORD

the Atlantic to the Urals) has for time immemorial been divided into two halves: one aligned to ancient Rome and the Catholic Church, the other to Byzantine and Orthodox Christianity. After 1945 the line dividing these two parts of Europe moved a few kilometres to the west and some nations which had always been considered a part of the West now found themselves to the east of that line." (Kundera: *Únos západu*).

The term postcolonialism is mostly used in relation to African and Asian countries; in literature it is used to describe works reflecting the state of societies recovering from years of oppression, subjection and underdevelopment. Although the word is also sometimes used in reference to the USA, it is rarely mentioned in reference to central Europe, however, despite the fact countries here came under Russian hegemony after the war. Slovak and Czech society were both exposed to such ideological pressure that the country lost its independence and its people their individual freedom: it was, in the words of B. Bakuła, a kind of cultural imperialism which prevailed here. After exposure of the Stalin cult of personality, Czechoslovakia started to turn more towards the West, a trend which led to the so-called Prague Spring. This liberating process was sharply curtailed, however, by Soviet tanks in August 1968 and then followed by the period of Normalization which lasted until the end of 1989.

Dobiáš is one of those people who, because of their religious convictions, tried to stand up to Soviet-style dictatorship. Together with the Nobel-prize winners Alexander Solzhenitsyn and Herta Müller, he is a representative of prison camp literature, as are the other Slovak writers Peter Juščák with his novel: *...a nezabudni na labute! (...And Don't Forget the Swans!)* and Pavol Rankov with the novel *Matky (Mothers)*. He is very adept at incorporating his negative experiences from prison into his work, describing them in an authentic and convincing manner. In a book of interviews with Anton Baláž, we read how Dobiáš was witness to executions during his imprisonment in Pankrác in Prague:

A LONG NIGHT'S STORIES

> *Since I received a long sentence, I was put in a cell near to those of the prisoners who had been sentenced to death. One early morning towards the end of autumn 1954, I heard them being taken out for execution, some of them by force. I could hear banging in the corridor and muffled yells. From the execution ground there came a lone yell: "Long live freedom!" And if my ears didn't deceive me, I also heard someone shout "Long live Stalin!" (Baláž: Vyniesť na svetlo dňa príbehy dlhej noci).*

The theme of imprisonment is addressed in many literary works, especially so in so-called postcolonial prose. The emergence of this type of novel reflects the shift in the second half of the 20th century away from modernism towards postmodernism (T. Pynchon, M. Kundera, I. Calvino, U. Eco). This is typified by a move back to the storytelling tradition and more realistic narrative structures. These authors were no longer writing for a small circle of people but for all kinds of readers and their prose works have a realism and political outreach that is key to the genre.

Postcolonial prose is characterized by certain thematic and temporal elements and in parallel with the postmodern, created conditions for a personal kind of prose dealing with themes which during the years of Socialism were sensitive or even strictly prohibited. In its content, postcolonial prose often focuses on personalities whom it had been forbidden to mention in a positive light (people such as Alexander Dubček or Zora Jesenská, the translator of *Doctor Zhivago* into Slovak, for example); or on various taboo themes (such as the ideological re-education of prostitutes at the end of the 1940s as treated in Anton Baláž's novel *The Camp of Fallen Women*). It is not a new term but its use in this context is a new one. For four years Prof. Bogusław Bakuła led research at the University of Adam Mickiewicz in Poznan into contemporary literature and culture of central Eastern Europe (Poland, Hungary, Slovakia and Ukraine) which aimed at "postcolonial discourse". It is thus a term which can be used in relation to this part of Europe and reflects the fact

AFTERWORD

that so much of it came under Soviet hegemony after the war. At times these countries had a kind of semi-colonial status; at others the Soviets were utterly imperialistic in their crushing of resistance (in Poland and Hungary in 1956 and in Czechoslovakia in 1968). Certain topics could not be written about under any circumstances: the murder of 25,000 Polish officers in and around the forests of Katyn by NKVD staff on the orders of Stalin, for instance or the Hungarian revolution of 1956 and the Prague Spring. And then everything changed after the withdrawal of Soviet troops from central Europe: works could suddenly be written criticizing the colonists and the barbaric practices which had become normal within the Socialist camp.

When considering literary works, we see how this theme has been addressed in many different ways. We may identify the following different types of prose:

1. The artistic political novel (such as Anton Baláž's *The Camp of Fallen Women*),
2. The biographical novel (such as Ľuboš Jurík's *Alexander Dubček / Rok dlhší ako storočie—A Year Longer than a Century*),
3. Biographical essays (Jozef Tóth's: Človek *Jób hovorí s diablom*),
4. The family novel (an example is the novel by the Polish author Andrzej Mularczyk: *Post mortem, Katyń*, the literary inspiration to the film by Andrzej Wajdu).
5. The crime novel (Rudolf Dobiáš: *Johana. Johanin chlapec*)
6. The 'GULAG novel' (Herta Müller's: *Atemschaukel,* Pavol Rankov: *Matky*, Peter Juščák: *... a nezabudni na labute!*)
7. Prose with a 'postmortal' character (the imaginary tale about the famous translator, Zora Jesenská, written by her husband, Ján Rozner and published under the title *Sedem dní do pohrebu—Seven Days till the Funeral*).

Of all these authors, only Tóth and Dobiáš have personal experience of being prisoners. Tóth is a Greek-Catholic priest who, like many other

Catholic intellectuals, became embroiled in complex socio-political events after 1948. Interned in a forced labour camp (a so-called PTP) in 1950, he called this period of his life his "black Sorbonne", meaning a "university" which many of the country's intelligentsia had passed through, people of integrity but deemed unreliable citizens by the political regime of the time. In his work *Človek Jób hovorí s diablom (Job Talks with the Devil)*, Tóth depicts the Devil as one of God's altar boys, a being who can only push the cart which God has created, an eternal parasite. Here Tóth metaphorically descends into the underworld in order to release love, faith, truth and hope from captivity. At the same time his work is a critical reaction to a regime which has decided to try and remove God from society through institutionalized atheism. Postcolonial prose is thus characterized by both symbolic and realistic elements and is written in response to very real political situations.

Dobiáš' crime novel *Johana. Johanin chlapec* is based on real events and its story develops serious themes in an engaging way. The author draws from real events in describing a village rebellion against collectivization, the murder of one of its organisers, the coercion of peasants into joining a cooperative farm and the condemnation of an innocent man. This man is Matej, husband of Johana and father of Ján. The story takes place near to a spa; as the author himself told me, he originally wanted to set it in Bardejov spa but then, after some deliberation, set it in Trenčianske Teplice and its surroundings instead, partly because he originates from and lives in Dobrá, which is part of Trenčianska Teplá and very close to the spa. The author took the two main characters, Matej and Johana, from real life. They are a traditional rural couple, the prototype for Johana being the author's own mother, a simple village woman with typical good qualities. Johana's son, a product of the marriage, is a boy who moves from Slovakia to Prague. The author puts himself into this character, primarily drawing in his depiction of Johana's son, Ján, from his own short stay in Prague after his seven-year imprisonment in the mines of Jáchymov.

AFTERWORD

After his release, Dobiáš visited Prague and thanks to Eman and Jan Zábran, met the poet Holan there in September 1960. In the novel the role of Holan is played by another real person, Jan Kristofori, originally a painter from Mukačevo, who also spent several years in the Jáchymov mines. Ján is helped by the painter during his stay in Prague but in 1968, Kristofori emigrates to Norway. This again shows that the author drew a lot of his ideas from his own prison experience though the painter from Mukačevo is the only real person in the novel who appears under his own name.

The novel is a crime story in which Matej is killed by the secret police as they investigate a murder. Matej is innocent—he merely found the dead body of the hated village functionary in the toilets. Also involved in the plot is the family of the Jewish spa doctor who Johana works for—and again we see Dobiáš drawing from his own personal experience, his mother having worked as a servant in the family of a Jewish doctor in Trenčianske Teplice from 1928 to 1932. In depicting the young woman reaching adulthood, the author challenges one of the dogmas of the Communist era: Johana felt at home with the Jewish family and was treated well; there is no hint that she was exploited and instead learnt much from them. Like many other Jewish doctors, bakers and traders, the family in the novel was deported from the Slovak state and sent to a concentration camp, a place from which very few Jewish families ever returned. Although the novel mainly focuses on the era of collectivization and its crime story is central, the tragedy of the holocaust and Slovakia's involvement in it are also touched on.

Given that Dobiáš draws from his prison experience in writing it, the novella *Temná zeleň (Deep Green)* can be classed as an example of prison camp literature. The main character is Celo (Celestín) Bizub, a former prisoner. The text has two narrative threads: one set in the 1950s and the uranium mines (1953-1960); the other in the late 1980s, when Celo meets with his former prison mate, Hoffart, or Kamagore as he was called. The two narratives constantly alternate and give the text a certain dynamism. The first storyline describes prison life and is richly autobiographical in its description of an attachment to a girl who came to visit a fellow prisoner, the anguish of a mother because of her son and then his return home from prison. All these are also described in Baláž's book *Vyniesť na svetlo dňa príbehy dlhej noci (Bring into the Daylight Tales of the Long Night)* The thread ends with an attempted escape by Kamagore and Celo, one only partly successful because while it seems Kamagore manages to escape, Celo twists his ankle and is unable to continue.

The second storyline begins with a telephone call from Bratislava thirty years later in which Kamagore, now an American citizen, invites Celo to Bratislava. There they meet up with some pretty girls, talk and drink but then fall out and separate in bad blood. After his return home, Celo is visited by members of the secret police asking him to identify the murdered Kamagore at the morgue in Bratislava; it is as if he is being punished for leaving his friend years before when they tried to escape from the camp. Thus Dobiáš combines a crime story with tales of imprisonment bringing to the text events which he himself experienced and has described elsewhere in his documentary prose.

Just as his novellas are authentic in the way they draw from his own experience, so are his short stories, notably *Cela (The Cell)* and *Hlad (Hunger)*. These could only have been written by someone with personal experience of imprisonment. In *Cela* he describes how he spends his day walking from the window of the cell to the door and back again; over sixteen hours, he calculates that he walks about sixty kilometres. In *Hlad*, he describes the chronic lack of food, a recurrent theme in prison camp literature and dominant in Herta Müller's *Atemschaukel (The Hunger Angel)* in which the gulag inmates suffer throughout. For Dobiáš, the shortage of food is very hard to deal with; as a young man, he needs a constant supply of energy. Someone helps him though, someone the author still remembers decades later.

AFTERWORD

We should also mention here the valuable work Dobiáš did as editor of a four-volume non-fiction document chronicling the fate of Slovak and Czech citizens imprisoned and even executed during the Communist years in Czechoslovakia. Their stories are told in an extensive series of short articles published under the title *Triedni nepriatelia (Class Enemies)* (published in 2004, 2007, 2011 and 2014). All totalitarian systems function through persecuting the so-called enemies within. German Fascists persecuted Jews, Communists members of higher classes (who they labelled 'exploiters of the working people') as well as representatives of the church. Thus well-to-do farmers (so-called *kulaks*), priests, bishops, nuns, doctors and businessmen were all amongst those persecuted by the new regime. In the four-volume publication, many of their tragic fates are described.

Dobiáš was interested in literature when still a student at *gymnázium* in Trenčín. As an eighteen-year old, he read a lot of poetry and particularly enjoyed the poems of Valentín Beniak, Rudolf Dilong and Andrej Žarnov. Beniak was his favourite, especially his poem *Spoveď v Santa Maria Maggiore (Confession in S.M.M.)*, which left a very deep impression on him largely because of its strong Christian feeling. Dobiáš also recalls Jáchymov in a collection of poems published in 2016 and titled *Noci a dni (Nights and Days)*. The most famous and affecting of these poems is *Kam odchádzate, jáchymovskí chlap ci? (Where are You Leaving Boys of Jáchymov?)*, a poem written as an obituary to another of the Jáchymov inmates, Štefan Paulíny. There are several similar poems in the collection mourning the deaths of his fellow prisoners—two of which are even referred to as 'requiems'. One poem is dedicated to Anton Srholec, a charismatic priest who Dobiáš befriended during his time in prison—the two spent several years together in the Jáchymov mines. These poems are deeply felt and describe life in the inhuman conditions of the uranium mines, a place where everyone was exposed to radioactivity. In other poems, the author declares his Christianity and draws on biblical motifs, at the same time enriching his verses with his own experiences—as he himself says—from 'out of the darkness'. The poet's religious convictions infuse all of his poems and were a source of great strength to him during the worst times of his long imprisonment. Until 1989 Dobiáš was a second-class citizen and as a writer, had to confine his work to prose and radio plays for children and young people. Later he emerged as an authentic voice of prison camp literature and possibly the only one to write about the uranium mines. His autobiography is mostly told in the book of interviews *Vyniesť na svetlo dňa príbehy dlhej noci (Bring into the Daylight Tales of the Long Night)*. Edited and published by Anton Baláž, the book is like a supplement to his life story. And it is a life story which not only testifies to the horrors of the Stalinist era but also provides great insight into totalitarianism and its mechanisms in general—as indeed does the whole literary output of Rudolf Dobiáš.

Tibor Žilka